The Hatching of Joshua Cobb

Other Books by Margaret Hodges

The Hatching of
JOSHUA COBB

by Margaret Hodges

ILLUSTRATED BY *W. T. Mars*

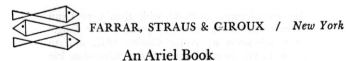

FARRAR, STRAUS & GIROUX / *New York*

An Ariel Book

Copyright © 1967 by Margaret Hodges
Third Printing, 1968
Library of Congress catalog card number: 67–19880
Printed in the United States of America
by American Book–Stratford Press, Inc.

Published simultaneously in Canada by
Ambassador Books, Ltd., Rexdale, Ontario

Designed by Irving Perkins

Acknowledgment is made with thanks to Lynn
Rohrbough for permission to quote "Canoe Song,"
from *Chansons de Notre Chalet*, 1957, and to
Anne C. Garrison for the original "Chocolate Pie
Song."

For
FLETCH, ART, JOHNNY *&* ANDY
who helped me remember the story

Contents

Contents

The Hatching of Joshua Cobb

ONE

Cabin 13, Camp Buddy

"My name is Warden," said the tall man. Behind him stood about a dozen young men. They were of various sizes and shapes, but to Josh they all looked huge and frightening. His stomach began to ache. Shuffling his feet, he moved closer to his mother.

"These are our counselors," Mr. Warden went on. "We've just been holding a final briefing before camp opens. And this is . . . ?" with a questioning look at Josh.

3

Josh stared at the floor and heard his mother say, "Joshua Cobb. He's called Josh. I'm his mother."

There was a short wait while Mr. Warden thumbed through a pile of applications and said cheerfully, "Here we are. Joshua Cobb. All right, Josh. You're going to be in Cabin 13 and your counselor is . . . let me see . . . Bert Bullock. Bert, here's your first boy. Take him over to Cabin 13 and see that he gets off to a good start."

Josh looked up, first at a pair of tough, hairy legs, then at a barrel chest covered with a tight white T-shirt, then at a broad red face topped by a mat of closely cropped red curls.

"Shouldn't I stay and help Josh unpack his things?" asked Mrs. Cobb.

"That won't be necessary," Mr. Warden told her. "Bert has plenty of time to help. Most of the boys are coming by bus and won't be here for a while. I wish we could ask you to stay for lunch, but the first meal is usually rather a rush. Don't feel you have to hurry off," he added politely.

Josh's mother got the message. A moment later, after a hasty kiss for Josh, she was gone, and Josh and Bert Bullock were lugging the new foot locker along a dirt path between a double line of cabins shaded by pine trees on the steep hillside. Looking down through branches, Josh saw lake water sparkling far below.

"Ye gods, what have you got in here?" said Bert. "Rocks?"

Panting and sweating under the rear end of the heavy load, Josh could only gasp, "I don't know. My mother packed it."

"Yeah," said Bert. "That figures. Mama's boy. You'll never use most of it. You staying two weeks, or four?"

"Two."

"If you last even that long," Bert said. "Which I doubt. Well, come on. Double time. Hup, two, three, four." He began to trot. Josh ran a few steps, trying to keep up. He stubbed his toe against the root of a pine tree and dropped his end of the foot locker.

"This end is the heaviest," he said.

"So?" said Bert. "Don't stand there. Pick it up. *Come* on."

Down the long path they went, buckety, buckety, Josh's arms straining in their sockets until Bert came to a sudden halt. The rear end of the foot locker thumped painfully against Josh's stomach.

"Here we are—Cabin 13, you lucky bum," Bert told him. "Left and *hup* the steps, two, three, four, and over here to the rear, two, three, four. Drop it."

The new foot locker dropped to the floor with a crash and Josh looked around him.

Cabin 13, like all the others, was built of pine boards that ended halfway up the walls. Above the low wooden walls, screening ran all around the cabin to let in air and to keep out bugs. Above the screening, canvas awnings were rolled up out of the way, ready to be let down in case of rain. Three double-decker bunks with bare mattresses were ranged around the walls and flanked with hooks and shelves.

By the front door, four charts were thumbtacked to the wall. The charts had squares for every day of camp, and there were columns labeled *Punctuality, Neatness.* . . . Josh did not take time to read all of the columns, but he saw his name at the top of one of the charts.

In the center of the cabin was a single bunk, on which Bert Bullock now sat down.

"All right, Cobb," he said. "Did your mother say they call you Corn Cobb?" He grinned at his own joke.

Josh winced inwardly. "They call me Josh," he said. He had already been called Corn Cobb a few times at school and didn't especially like it. It made him feel uneasy to have a nickname he hadn't picked out for himself, as if more teasing might follow, more teasing than he wanted.

"Well, Corn Cobb," Bert said, "get going. Open up that foot locker and put the things you need on

6

your hooks and shelves. You're in the top bunk at the rear. Put your sleeping bag on your mattress and spread it out neatly. There will be four guys here for sure, and maybe six. I'm going to run a tight ship."

Josh was on his knees opening the foot locker. "I didn't bring a sleeping bag," he said. "The list didn't say to bring a sleeping bag."

"They must have sent you an old list," Bert told him. "Everybody brings sleeping bags. They must have forgotten to tell you. What *did* you bring?"

"Sheets and blankets," Josh said apologetically.

"Well, it's your funeral," said Bert. "Ever make a bed in a top bunk with sheets and blankets?" He grinned again. "You'll learn." Then he leaned over and peered at the raised lid of the foot locker. Inside the lid Joshua's mother had pasted a neatly typed list of everything that the locker contained. Bert snorted with laughter. "Ye gods! 'Two blankets, four sheets, four pillow cases, three pajamas . . .'"

In Josh's foot locker was every item that had been mentioned on Camp Buddy's list of REQUIRED CLOTHING AND EQUIPMENT, besides all the things on the list of OPTIONAL CLOTHING AND EQUIPMENT and a good many other things that Joshua's mother had thought of. There were extra galoshes in case he lost the first pair, sunburn lotion, mosquito spray, Band-Aids, poison-ivy lotion, and even a small bottle of aspirin in case of a headache or a sniffle.

7

Bert read down the whole list. Too much of everything a camper wouldn't need—and no sleeping bag, the most important thing! Just Josh's luck! He was afraid to ask Bert to let him sleep in a lower bunk where it would be easier to make up a bed with sheets and blankets.

"You've got enough for an army," Bert said. "Unpack one of everything and leave the rest in your locker. Shove it under the bunk."

But before Josh could follow these orders, he had to unpack the locker to the very bottom. He was still squatting in the midst of heaped-up clothing when he heard a heavy motor groan to a stop in the distance. Soon afterward the screen door banged open and two other campers came in, announcing that they had been assigned to Cabin 13. They gave their names as John Morris and Greg Jones.

Listening to the conversation, Josh learned that this was their second year at camp. He also learned that Bert Bullock had never been a counselor before. Bert was busy issuing orders to John and Greg. He left Josh in peace to sort out his belongings, but Josh was too much interested in the other boys to make a very good job of it.

John Morris was about Josh's size. He looked neat and serious, and Josh could see that John had what Josh's school called "good coordination." Josh did not have it. He guessed that John Morris would be

8

good at tennis and baseball and would know how to swim without keeping one foot on the bottom. This was something that bothered Josh a lot. It was a secret known, he hoped, only to himself and his mother. He *had* to keep one foot on the bottom when he swam. Here at Camp Buddy his fear of deep water would be discovered, and then what would he do?

Josh had another reason for being dissatisfied with himself. He knew that his mother did too many things for him at home. His father had died when Josh was a baby and his mother had tried to be both mother and father to him. During the three-hour drive to camp she had talked about it. "I know I do too many things for you, Josh. I don't mean to, but I do. You're ten years old and it's time for you to start taking a little responsibility for yourself."

Thinking of this, he watched with respect while Morris laid out a sleeping bag on a lower bunk and unpacked his small duffel bag with speed and precision.

Greg Jones was a lot taller than Josh and much fatter. His face was like a full moon. He was perspiring freely now as he knelt before his suitcase, unpacking at a snail's pace under Bert's impatient directions.

"Hey, Jones, get a move on. What do they call you, anyway? Jumbo? Jumbo Jones, that has to be it.

10

Get your stuff stowed away there, Jumbo. You'll have to move faster than that if you don't want to have a lot of holes in your chart." He turned to look again at Josh, who had managed to put a few things, chosen at random, into his storage space and to slam the locker lid shut on a tumbled heap of everything else.

"Shove that under before I give you a knuckle rub," Bert ordered. "There's at least one more guy to come, and he'll sleep below you. This is Corn Cobb," he told the other two boys. "Corn Cobb, meet Jumbo Jones and . . . and Boris Morris."

The three boys looked at each other without smiling or shaking hands, united only by their common fate as members of Cabin 13. They eyed Bert warily. He sounded tough and mean, but some big guys sounded like that and then turned out all right after all.

"And here comes another lucky guy for Cabin 13," said Bert, as the door opened again. The boy who came in was bent under a duffel bag carried on his shoulders. His face was invisible under a mop of long black hair until he dropped the duffel bag and stood up, tossing his hair back out of his eyes. He was tall and thin as a rail.

"Spears!" chorused Boris and Jumbo. (Already Bert's nicknames were fixed in Josh's mind.) "Spears! Hey, there!" So, this was another old Camp

11

Buddy boy. Josh was the only new boy in Cabin 13. The old boys outnumbered him three to one, though in fact the old boys felt almost like strangers, too, if Josh had only known it. Faces look different from one summer to the next, and camp friendships have to be made all over again each year.

The tall boy handed Bert a slip of paper. Bert read it, frowning. "Spears, eh?" he said. "And Warden says here that there will just be the four of you. The other two have canceled. So that's the whole ball of wax—Cobb, Morris, Jones, and Spears. Spider Spears."

"His name's David," said Boris Morris.

"His name's Spider," said Bert.

Four pairs of eyes now looked up at Bert Bullock, then at each other. What kind of a counselor was this? Friend—or enemy?

TWO

In Starving Condition

"Do you like Bert?" mumbled Jumbo, formerly Greg Jones, now Jumbo, by Bert's decree. He and Josh were going down the long steep path from the camp to the lake.

"What?" said Josh. At the moment he could think of nothing but the pain of walking barefoot on pebbles. Josh had never gone barefoot much and his feet were tender. Far below, already standing with a crowd of other boys on the dock, he saw Boris and

13

Spider, who had run down the path as quickly and easily as if it had been covered with a soft rug, or as if they had hoofs instead of feet. Jumbo did not like to run and was glad for an excuse to walk down slowly with Josh, even if they were the last ones in for a swim.

"I said, do you like Bert?" Jumbo repeated.

"I don't know yet," Josh answered, but he did know. He could not forget Bert at supper last night, doling out small spoonfuls of stew to the boys at his table and eating almost a bowlful himself. He could not forget the sting of Bert's towel snapped at his bare legs to make him hurry to bed. Or Bert's growl soon afterward, "All right, you guys—quiet! Anyone who talks gets a knuckle rub!" Bert's knuckle rubs were already famous in Cabin 13. He would double up his big fist, seize a boy's head under his elbow as if it were a football, and massage it painfully.

"My counselor last year wasn't like that," said Jumbo. "If he had been, I wouldn't have come back."

Down below, on the lake front, a whistle blew. "We'd better hurry," Jumbo told Josh. "That's Kenny's whistle—he's the swimming counselor— and there's Bert with his towel." Hobbling and teetering on the sharp stones, Josh stumbled after Jumbo to join the crowd.

A fresh breeze was blowing across the lake. Two

14

slender canoes were being launched by a pair of counselors, the paddles dripping and shining as they manuevered away from the dock. The campers shivered and squinted into the morning sunshine. The swimming counselor, feet apart, hands on hips, looked them over like a naval officer.

"Now hear this!" he barked. "All you guys who were here last year, how many of you were Whales?"

About twenty hands went up. "Take a buddy," ordered the swimming counselor, "and go on in at the deep end." The Whales paired off and dived, two by two, from the far end of the dock.

"Now, who was a Sailfish last year?"

Many hands were waved in air.

"Take a buddy," ordered the counselor, "and go in off the side."

There was a scramble as the Sailfish found buddies and disappeared off the side of the dock, some diving, some jumping, to bob up splashing and shouting a second later in the clear cold water that was neck-deep for most of them at that spot. Boris and Spider were both Sailfish.

Kenny the counselor surveyed the crowd of boys still standing on the dock. "All right," he said, "the rest of you were Minnows last year, right? Or else you're new boys. Come on, take a buddy and get into the Tank. When you hear me yell 'Buddy!,' find your buddy and hold on to him. If you were

here last year, you ought to remember. If you're new, don't forget, or you'll be pulled out of the water. Now let's see you swim."

"Be my buddy," said Jumbo. Josh nodded gratefully. Below the dock, where the water was shallow, he saw a wooden frame that made a sort of pool. One by one the Minnows climbed down a ladder into the Tank and found the water only waist-deep. Kenny blew the whistle and shouted "Buddy!" At the end of the dock and all around it, pairs of boys clasped hands and held them in the air. Kenny frowned down at the Minnows in the Tank. "Not bad," he said briefly. "All right, swim!"

As the swimming began again all around the dock, the Minnows did their best, keeping one eye on Kenny. He looked down at them without expression while they floundered about. Josh swam from one end of the Tank to the other, keeping one foot on the bottom and hoping for the best. Suddenly above him on the dock he heard Bert Bullock's voice. "That's Cobb. I've got him in my cabin. I didn't think he could swim, and he can't. He can't play baseball either. Probably can't do anything."

Josh continued to pretend to swim as if he had not heard. Without knowing it, Bert had just voiced Josh's own opinion of himself. He had found out yesterday on the ball field that Josh couldn't bat and couldn't catch. There was no way to hide that. But

17

Josh had hoped that his foot, reassuringly touching bottom in the Tank, would not show and that he could somehow get through camp without having to face his fear of the water. Now Bert had found out that secret. And there was more to come. Bert would find out that Josh couldn't play tennis, either. At school everyone knew he wasn't good at sports, but it didn't matter. Josh could do other things. He could do science experiments and tell good jokes. He could think up ideas for skits. He photographed everybody in his class and gave away the pictures. Everybody liked him at school, as far as he knew. Camp might be different. Sports really mattered a lot here, and so did many other things that he did not do well at home. But when he didn't make his bed right at home, no one snapped a towel at him. If he left his clothes on the floor, no one gave him a knuckle rub. If he was not on time, his mother sighed, but she didn't growl. Above all, if his side lost a game at school, it was not fatal, because the teams were always being changed. Nobody had to be stuck with Josh all the time, so nobody was sure he was a jinx—except Josh himself. When sides were chosen for a game, Josh knew he would be chosen last, but no one held that against him.

Now he belonged to the Indian team at Camp Buddy, and he would be an Indian as long as he was at camp. They were stuck with him for good. He

would never win a single point for the Indians, and when the points were counted up at the end of camp, everyone would know why the Pioneers had won. It would be all the fault of Josh Cobb. He would have earned the nickname, Corn Cobb, and there was not a single thing he could do about it.

"Minnows out!" shouted Kenny. "Back to your cabins on the double!" Josh clambered up the wooden ladder and followed Jumbo up the steep path at the end of a long line of Minnows. The pebbles hurt so much that Josh began to count his steps. After fifty steps the cabins were still far above him and he changed to a marching verse which had sometimes stood him in good stead:

> Left, left, left my wife and ninety-nine children
> At home in bed in starving condition
> With nothing but gingerbread left, left . . .

"What?" said Jumbo. He turned around, red and panting. "What did you say?"

"Left," said Josh.

> Left, left my wife and ninety-eight children
> At home in bed in starving condition
> With nothing but gingerbread left, left . . .

Jumbo chortled. "That's good," he said. "How does it go? Left, left . . ."

19

Chanting and marching in time, they reached the top of the hill. The rest of the Minnows had already disappeared into their cabins to dress for lunch. Josh and Jumbo ran along the path, spattered with sun and shade, toward Cabin 13.

"Maybe we won't be Minnows pretty soon," said Jumbo. "Kenny gives a test, and if you pass it, you're a Sailfish. I think I can pass it. I almost could last summer. Swimming's more fun than baseball—and all like such. The best thing is when you get to be a Whale. That's when they let you go out in a canoe."

Josh did not answer. Canoeing seemed impossibly remote for a Minnow who swam with one foot touching bottom. He ran up the steps into Cabin 13 and began to dress. It would have been more comfortable to have another new boy in the cabin, he thought. It made him feel out of things to be the only new one. All around on the walls and ceiling were the jokes of other summers scrawled in black ink or poster paint: SCHEME. FLUNK NOW, AVOID THE RUSH LATER. KEEP TENSE. DON'T GO AWAY MAD, JUST GO AWAY. DRACULA SLEEPS HERE.

"Who was Dracula?" he asked Jumbo as he pulled on his T-shirt.

"Dracula?" said Jumbo, puffing over his shoelaces. "Oh, that was our counselor last year, the night of the Ghost Hike. That was funny. I wish we had him again."

20

The steps creaked and Bert Bullock came in. "Who do you wish you had again?" he said. He looked suspiciously from Jumbo to Josh. "Pair of soreheads, eh?" They did not answer, and a moment later he turned his attention to Boris and Spider, who came running along the path with the other Sailfish. "Step on it, you guys. If you're late for lunch, you'll get a knuckle rub."

Well, thought Josh, at least Bert Bullock was not singling him out from the rest. He was just the same way to all of them, and that way was—mean.

After lunch Mr. Warden handed out the mail. Josh had a long letter from his mother. He read it three times from beginning to end and carried it in his pocket for the rest of the day.

THREE

Corn Cobb

Josh was sitting at the end of a bench under a tree. Before him the big sports field baked in the heat of the mid-afternoon sun. The scrub baseball teams were playing at one side of the field under the direction of Bert Bullock. It seemed more like work than play, Josh thought. He was the only one from Cabin 13 who had to play today with the scrubs. Boris Morris was so good that he played with the All-Stars. Jumbo had a sore toe, or so he said. Spider was

already on a "farm team" and he would be promoted to play with the older All-Stars this summer, if Josh didn't miss his guess. Spider had natural style in baseball. It seemed to Josh that Spider could catch anything, whether it was really coming his way or not, and he had already made two home runs in the two days since camp had started.

The "farm teams" occupied the far side of the field, where they seemed to be enjoying themselves. Josh could see a tall gangling counselor stretched out on the ground near the other diamond, chewing a blade of grass. Now and then he seemed to cock a friendly eye at the farm-team game, but his style of coaching was nothing like Bert's. Bert was running in place, breaking in a pair of new football shoes and shouting at the scrub-team boys. These unfortunates were the youngest boys—and Josh, who was a candidate for the All-Goofs, according to Bert. Bert called him Corn Cobb all the time now, but nobody else did. Josh guessed they must think he couldn't take it. He sat down at the end of the bench with a faint hope that the inning might end before he would have to bat.

"You out there at second base," yelled Bert, "watch the game! What are you going to do if someone starts to run bases?—which I doubt." Second base scampered back to his post and crouched over it dutifully.

A wiry little boy, who looked younger than Josh, stepped up to bat. The pitcher threw a wobbly ball. "Not underarm, stupid," yelled Bert. "What did I tell you?" He came to a halt in his running, examined the soles of his shoes with dissatisfaction, and mopped his red face with the sleeve of his T-shirt.

The pitcher, glancing nervously at Bert, threw again and there was a clean hard crack as the bat connected with the ball. The wiry little batter raced toward first base, while the ball sailed off to the other side of the field. Spider Spears scooped it up as it skittered toward him over the dry grass. Then he threw the ball to the nearest boy in the scrub-team outfield. It was almost an insult. Why couldn't he just let the scrub team get their own ball? That was Spider all over, thought Josh, watching from his bench. Spider was good at everything and wanted you to know it. Boris was good too, but he did not brag. Spider bragged all the time, about baseball and about swimming and about his father's big new car. It seemed to be the only way he knew how to talk. That was one thing Josh did not do, he said to himself. He never bragged. But then he didn't have anything to brag *about*.

Bert was running in place again. He was going to college in the fall and he expected to go out for ball. At dinner last night he had told the inmates 13 that Camp Buddy was a good chance to

get in shape for football. That was why Bert needed a lot of food. He told them about that as he served up one hot dog for each boy and three for himself. There were beans too—what looked like about one bean for each boy and a whole plateful for Bert. He did not suggest getting more from the kitchen until he had finished eating his last bean. By that time it was too late for second helpings, but the boys were afraid to complain.

At bedtime last night Josh had written to his mother: "Dear Mother, How are you? I am fine. Camp is a lot of fun. There are two teams, the Pioneers and the Indians. I am an Indian and we are in second place, so far. You were right, there are inspections at this camp. Every boy has a chart and you get points for neatness and for being on time and like that. Bert Bullock is our counselor. If you make a mistake, he puts a hole in your chart. You get the Eagle for the neatest cabin and the Skunk for the messiest cabin. We got the Skunk yesterday. It was mostly my fault. You get the Pot of Gold for the best table manners and the Pig for the worst table manners. Please send me a sleeping bag and a cherry pie. You can mark it FRAGILE. And write to me soon. Josh."

Sitting out on the bench by the field, Josh could not remember when he had been so hungry. And had only been at Camp Buddy for two days!

was he going to last for two weeks? Visions of his mother's cherry pie floated before him, its crust so brown and tender and flaky with the juice bubbling up from inside, and the cherries plump, tart, and sweet between his teeth. Josh's mouth watered.

"Corn Cobb!" yelled Bert Bullock. "You're at bat. What are you, blind?"

Josh rose reluctantly. He stepped out into the sun and picked up the bat. There was the wiry little boy, already at third base. Someone had got to second while Josh had been dreaming of cherry pie. Yes, there was a runner at first, too. The bases were loaded and Josh knew perfectly well what would happen next. The pitcher threw a fast one and Josh swung.

"Strike one!" shouted Bert.

Josh tapped home plate and waggled the bat, praying for a miracle. It was not to be.

"Strike two!"

All over the diamond the runners were calling, "Hit it! Hit it! Come on, Cobb!" Josh swung.

"Strike three!" said Bert, looking at Josh in disgust. "You did great, Cobb, just great. All right, you guys. Keep the game going. I'll be back."

As the new inning started, Bert trotted off toward the counselors' hut, glancing at his watch. His parting shot was, "Good old Corn Cobb, greatest living relative of Ty Cobb!"

On his way to his usual place in the outfield, where no balls were likely to come, Josh set his teeth. It was bad enough to strike out with the bases loaded. Why did Bert have to ride him like that? But as it turned out, Bert's comments were a blessing in disguise. Whatever uncomplimentary things the three runners might have said to Josh before, they did not say them now. Nobody wanted to put himself in a class with Bert Bullock. In any case, it was perfectly clear to every other boy that Josh had done his best. Anyone could strike out. The wiry little boy booed at Bert's retreating back, but Bert did not look around. He probably thought the "boo" was meant for Josh.

With Bert gone, the game was a lot more fun. Josh wondered vaguely why Bert seemed to have so many duties in the counselors' hut, especially before supper and before bedtime. Still, it was certainly all right with Josh. Life in Cabin 13 was more peaceful when Bert was busy somewhere else.

The farm teams' game was ending with cheers and Josh saw those boys coming across the field with Dusty Moore, the tall gangling counselor. They were talking and laughing about something. Everyone looked happy and relaxed. The tall counselor paused in the shade at the edge of the field.

"Come on, Dusty," said one of the farm-team boys. "We don't want to watch the scrubs."

"Most of you were scrubs last year, remember?" said Dusty. "I want to watch them. They might have some good material."

Josh was just near enough to hear the words. He thought he would like to catch a ball for once, while that tall counselor, Dusty, was watching. He dodged back and forth whenever he thought a ball might be coming his way, but someone else always managed to get it first. After a while Dusty went away and the Get Ready bell rang for supper. The scrub-team boys straggled off to their cabins.

Josh found Jumbo, Spider, and Boris lying on their bunks, reading comic books. They had already washed in the Soap Palace, the long, low building where everybody had to take a shower before supper.

"You'd better hurry," said Boris. "If you're late, you know what Red Bull will do."

Red Bull! That was a perfect nickname, all right. Josh wondered if Bert had heard it yet. He snatched his towel and hurried off to the Soap Palace. When he came back, the others had gone to the dining hall, and on the ceiling above Bert's bunk someone had painted a new motto: HONESTY IS THE ROAD TO STAR-VATION. Someone had a lot of nerve, thought Josh. Was it Jumbo? Spider? Boris?

Feeling hollow, he raced all the way to the dining hall, but he was late. Everyone was eating and the

only empty place was at the end of the table next to Bert, who handed out a verdict and a plate at the same time. "Corn Cobb, you get a hole in your chart for being late."

On the plate was a small spoonful of macaroni and a mountain of sliced beets. Josh guessed correctly that Red Bull did not like beets. Josh did not much like beets either, but he ate them, down to the very last one.

That night he wrote a postcard to his mother. "Dear Mother: When is the cherry pie coming? Send it soon. Your son, Josh."

31

only empty place was at the end of the table next to
Jerry, who handed out a verdict and a plate at the
same time. "Claire Cobb, you get a hole in your chair
for being late."

On the plate was a small spoonful of macaroni and
a mountain of sliced beets. Josh guessed correctly
that Red Bull did not like beets. Josh did not much
like beets either, but he ate them, down to the very
last one.

That night he wrote a postcard to his mother.
"Dear Mother, When is the cherry pie coming? Send
it soon. Your son, Josh."

FOUR

The Skunk Award

Right after breakfast at Camp Buddy, while everyone was still sitting at the table in the big dining hall, Mr. Warden stood up and made all the announcements for the day. Josh did not think much of Camp Buddy breakfasts; juice poured from big cans, boxes of cold cereal standing on the tables, baskets of toast or buns that were always cold by the time you ate them, and pitchers of lukewarm milk. It was not like breakfast at home, where Josh's

mother brought him everything, ice cold or piping
hot, whichever it should be, just when he was ready
to eat it.

Still, it was fun to eat with so many boys. Josh
knew that Jumbo Jones was already a real friend,
and he admired Boris Morris more than almost any
boy he had ever met. Boris was very serious and he
did not say much, but everything he did was exactly
right. He was the best athlete in Cabin 13, his
clothes were always neat, and everything he owned
was always where it should be. Nothing ever seemed
to bother him. Josh did not feel that he knew Boris
as well as he knew Jumbo and Spider. He hoped he
would know him well before camp was over.

Boris had just won the right to go out in a canoe.
He now wore a silver pin on the pocket of his T-
shirt, a pair of crossed paddles. A real pair of crossed
paddles hung on the wall of the dining hall behind
Mr. Warden's head as he stood up to make the
announcements. On a shelf under the paddles were
all the camp trophies, silver cups, inscribed year
after year with the names of winners.

Josh was thinking about all this as Mr. Warden
talked. There would be tennis lessons for the new
boys that morning before swimming. (Josh groaned
inwardly. He knew he was going to be hopeless at
tennis before he even started, but at least Bert Bullock did not coach tennis.) In the afternoon the
Indians would go to the big field for a track meet.

"And tomorrow," concluded Mr. Warden, "there will be a Treasure Hunt in the woods. More about that later." Cheers and clapping greeted this announcement. "Now for inspection reports." He nodded to the head counselor, who stood up in his place, looking over the reports that had been handed to him during breakfast.

"Cabins are shaping up pretty well," said the head counselor. "Most of you who were here last year seem to be remembering what you learned. And if you're new, you're learning fast. Today the Eagle goes to—Cabin 5." Cheers and clapping. "The Skunk again goes to—Cabin 13." Boos, cheers, and clapping. "Someone in Cabin 13 left his swimming suit under his bunk and one of the top bunks was a mess."

The head counselor sat down. Bert glowered at Josh. "Must have been your bunk," he said. Josh could already feel the knuckle rub that Bert would give him the next time he caught him. But who had left the swimming suit under a bunk? Josh knew he had hung his on the line behind the cabin. He looked at the other three boys, who shrugged and looked uneasily at Bert.

The moment Mr. Warden gave the word "Dismissed," all four of the boys raced from the dining hall to the morning's activities before Bert could express his wrath. They did not see him again until the morning swim, when, surprisingly, he said noth-

ing about the Skunk award. Bert never dealt out knuckle rubs when other counselors were around. He saved them for the privacy of Cabin 13.

Josh's feet were still painful on the long path down to the lake, but this morning he was hardly conscious of them. He was concentrating on how well he might do today in the Tank with the other Minnows. Every day Kenny, the swimming counselor, made them hold on to the side of the Tank and kick. Then he made them put their faces under water and blow bubbles. They had to practice some strokes, too, standing in the water. Then they were allowed to splash around and play. All at once, yesterday, Josh had realized that the water was fun. Instead of thinking that he was going to drown, he had begun to look enviously at the Sailfish swimming in deeper water.

Today again, after the first cool shock, the lake seemed almost warm. The sun was burning his bare shoulders. The summer breeze caressed his face, sent little clouds sailing across the blue sky, lightly stirred the tops of the pine trees. Far out on the lake, two of the senior campers were paddling a canoe, their oars dipping and swinging. The air smelled different from city air. Josh felt wonderful. He waded to the middle of the Tank, flung himself on the water and struck out, arms and legs flailing, for

the edge. He had swum several strokes before his legs sank to the bottom. Smiling, sputtering, Josh stood up and looked around. No one had seen him swimming. The other Minnows were too busy with their own attempts. Kenny was on the dock, looking the other way. But Josh had done it! He had really swum without one foot on the bottom, and he knew he could do it again. He would swim farther next time. Tomorrow maybe he would swim clear across the Tank.

Swimming was funny, he thought. You had to believe you could do it before you could swim, and you could not believe it—at least Josh couldn't— until you did swim. It was a wonder he had ever got a start! Again and again he launched out for the edge, thrashing wildly. Even when he choked on a mouthful of water, he did not stop until the whistle blew.

Josh and Jumbo brought up the rear as the Minnows climbed the hill. Someone halfway up the line turned and called back, "Hey, Cobb, how does that go? Left, left . . ."

Jumbo and Josh grinned at each other and chanted together:

Left, left, left my wife and ninety-nine children
At home in bed in starving condition
With nothing but gingerbread left . . .

One after another the Minnows took up the words until they echoed across the lake. Josh had not had such a good time since camp began. In spite of the tennis lesson, which had turned out even worse than he had expected, this was the best morning yet. All at once something whizzed behind him. He felt a sharp sting across the back of his legs. Another whiz and a yelp from Jumbo. They turned and saw Bert Bullock ready to snap his towel at them again. Jumbo's face crumpled. "Don't," he said. "Please don't."

"Who wrote on the ceiling above my bed?" said Bert.

"Not me," said Jumbo. "Please don't snap at my legs. It hurts."

"That's good for you," Bert said. He passed them at a run, heading for the cabin. None of the other boys had seen him snapping his towel. That was how Bert was.

"Why did we have to get him for our counselor?" muttered Jumbo. "I'm not having any fun this year. I can't stand him."

"I don't think he likes us much either," said Josh. "All he really wants to do is to get in shape for football. And you know what? I think he was the one who left that swimming suit under a bunk. He's not so neat himself, and all the time he's punching our charts full of holes—all except Boris."

39

"And why does he leave us every night?" complained Jumbo. "My counselor last year didn't do that. He used to read to us, and it was fun. Old Red Bull just tells us to shut up and off he goes. I'm not going to stand it much longer. I'll go home. That's what I'll do."

"Don't do that," said Josh. "It wouldn't be the same if you went. Why don't we tell Mr. Warden?"

"The Establishment?" said Jumbo. "No one ever tells the Establishment anything."

"What's the Establishment?" asked Josh.

"The people that run things," said Jumbo. "Mr. Warden and the nurse and the cook, and—and all like such. They're always the last to know anything that goes wrong, because no one ever tells."

Josh pondered this bit of wisdom as they reached the top of the hill and began to walk toward Cabin 13. "Why doesn't anyone ever tell?" he asked.

"Because," said Jumbo. "The boys don't tell because they don't want to be chicken. And the counselors don't tell because they always stick together. But last year nothing went wrong except little things, and all the counselors were nice."

They dressed for lunch silently and at top speed. Neither of them wanted to be late in the dining hall, and both of them already had several holes in their charts for not being on time. It was not until Josh pulled on his socks that he noticed the soles of his

feet. They seemed to be toughening up a little. Anyway, he had not thought about them once on the path up from the lake this time. Probably that was because he had so many other things to think about, some good, some bad.

FIVE

One Shoe Off and One Shoe On

About half of the campers were gathered at one end of the big field for a track meet, and Dusty Moore, the track counselor, was dividing them into two teams, handing out green or gray badges to be pinned on shirt fronts—green badges for Indians, gray for Pioneers. He called the older boys first, referring to a list.

"All right, you fellows," he said, "let's start with a relay race to the flagpole and back. I guess you're

43

about even as far as size goes. And anyway, size doesn't matter much." He dug two starting lines in the dirt with his heel and handed out two batons. "Ready!" he called. "Get set! Go!"

Two of the senior runners raced off toward the flagpole with the sound of cheers and shouts following them. The second runners stood ready to take the batons. Under the trees at the edge of the field, Josh watched with the younger boys. He liked Dusty Moore and he did not mind running. He had always run fairly well at school and he thought he could probably do all right now. Maybe the Indians would not be too sorry that he was on their side this afternoon. Boris Morris was an Indian too, and Spider Spears was a Pioneer. Jumbo was not there at all. He said he had a headache. At the end of camp there would be a final track meet, Pioneers against Indians.

The relay race for the older boys ended with an Indian victory. "Come on, you juniors," called Dusty. "Let's see what you can do. Same race, to the flagpole and back." The junior boys, divided into two teams under Dusty's orders, trotted out to the starting lines.

Spider grinned and called over from the Gray lineup, "Yay! We're going to beat you!" He was the last runner for the Grays.

"There are twelve on each side," Boris said to

Josh. "I want to be last. You go next to last, right before me. Be sure not to drop the stick."

"I won't," said Josh. He lined up in front of Boris and the race began. The first pair of runners reached the flagpole, touched it, and raced back, neck and neck. The second pair started off, batons held tightly, and ran back still evenly matched. Even the seniors were yelling now. The junior relay race was going to be an exciting one. From their places on the sidelines the older boys were shouting, "Come on, Greens! Come on, you Grays! Run!"

A Gray runner pulled ahead and came back a good five yards before the matching Green. Josh was jumping up and down. "Come on, Greens! Beat 'em!" It would soon be his turn. He felt himself tensing up. But there was Dusty Moore, chewing a piece of grass and calling out, "Keep loose!" Josh relaxed.

The runner in front of him had reached the flagpole. He was gaining on the Gray runner. Here he came! Josh toed the mark. He stretched out his hand to catch the baton. He heard Boris yell, "Run!" And Josh ran. He ran halfway to the flagpole—and off flew the sneaker from his right foot. He stumbled, righted himself, and ran on without the sneaker, but it was no good with one shoe off and one shoe on. The gap widened between him and his Gray opponent. Spider, the last Gray runner, had the baton

and was off like a shot before Josh could reach the finish line and hand the baton to Boris. He was too humiliated even to watch the end of the race. A cheer went up from the Grays, while the Greens groaned. Well, he had lost the race for the Greens. And there was Bert Bullock standing by Dusty. Why did he have to turn up just at that moment?

"That's Corn Cobb for you," said Bert. "Can't even tie his shoes."

Josh ran back to pick up his sneaker, not looking at anyone. He thrust his foot into the sneaker and stumped over to the sidelines. What was the use? He was a loser, no matter what he tried to do. He sat in the grass, pretending to study the ants that were running in and out of a hole in the ground between his feet.

"Tough luck," said Spider, sitting down beside him. But he sounded pleased and Josh did not look up.

The seniors ran a hundred-yard dash and Josh did not even watch that race or any of those that followed. Then Dusty was calling, "Juniors ready for the fifty-yard dash." Josh did not move.

Dusty went on with a few pointers as the juniors gathered at the mark. "Your starts are very important. Always try to do some practice starts before you race. Work your arms straight up and down with your elbows close to your sides. Don't let your arms

crisscross in front of you. Run on your toes, not on your heels. And at the end of the race, don't lie down. Jog around for a while to keep your muscles from getting stiff. And don't be scared if you get sick. That sometimes happens after a race. It doesn't mean anything."

Josh, who had been feeling sick, looked up.

"Come on, Cobb," called Dusty. "You're in this race." Josh shook his head. Dusty walked over to him and pulled him to his feet. "Come on," he said cheerfully. "Anyone can lose a shoe. Tie it tight this time."

Josh hesitated. Then he knelt down and tied a double knot in each shoelace. He took a deep breath and jogged over to the starting mark. Two of the seniors ran to the flagpole with a tape for the finish line.

"Two heats in this race," said Dusty. "We'll run you twelve at a time. First the Greens, then the Grays. Then the three winners from each side will race each other for the finals. Greens at the starting line!"

Josh lined up with the other Greens. He felt better when he saw that Bert had gone. Maybe he could do all right this time.

"On your mark! Get set! Go!" called Dusty, and away they went.

Out of the corner of his eye Josh could see Boris

running easily. He was neck and neck with Boris, well out in front of all the others. Then almost at the finish line someone came from behind like a small steam engine. It was the wiry little boy who had got to third base before Josh had struck out yesterday. He passed Josh and Boris as if they had been standing still. Boris put on a final burst of speed and came in second. Josh took third. Still, not so bad, he thought, as he jogged back to the sidelines. Not hopeless, anyway.

Spider came in second among the Grays' three winners, his arms and legs working like pistons. It seemed no time at all until Dusty was lining them up for the final heat of the junior fifty-yard dash. None of the finalists had had much of a rest. They looked at one another speculatively, wondering if they could last to the finish line. Josh felt tied up in knots. Then he remembered Dusty's advice, "Keep loose." He would try to.

On the word "Go!" they were off. The finish line looked twice as far off as before. Josh's breath came in gasps. His legs were like lead. A side glance showed him the other runners, all about even. No, there was the little baseball player putting on speed. He was the one to catch. And all at once Josh found his second wind. He'd catch that little guy or die trying! It turned out to be no problem. Twenty

49

yards from the goal the guy seemed to run out of fuel. His arms came down to his sides. He wobbled and sagged. Josh passed him with a clear field ahead. Then on his other side, long arms and legs appeared —Spider Spears, with more speed than Josh could match, Spider flinging himself across the finish line and sprawling on the grass. Dumfounded, Josh hesitated, broke his stride, and in that second, Boris passed him too. Above all the cheering and shouting, Dusty Moore called out, "Spears first, Morris second, Cobb third."

The juniors trotted back to their cabins just as the Get Ready bell rang for supper. Josh's heart was still pounding. He felt almost too tired to eat. But as he came into Cabin 13 Jumbo rolled over on his bunk to say, "You've got a package, Josh. It's marked FRAGILE."

Josh saw the package lying on his own bunk. His appetite came back with a rush. But oddly enough, much as he had longed for that package, it did not seem as important right now as the fact that he had taken third place in the fifty-yard dash. And even better, Cabin 13 had taken first, second, and third. Cabin 13 might be Skunks, but they were the fastest Skunks in camp!

"What's in your package?" asked Boris.

"It's a cherry pie," Josh told him.

"Hide it," said Spider, "or old Red Bull will eat it." Josh hid the package under his blankets.

"Can I have some tonight?" said Jumbo. "Because I'm leaving tomorrow."

SIX

Clues

"But *why* are you leaving?" asked Boris for the third time that evening. It was after Taps and Lights Out, but private conversation was easy under cover of the crickets in shrill chorus all over the Camp Buddy hilltop.

The inmates of Cabin 13 were lying in their bunks eating brownies, which had turned out to be the contents of Josh's package from home. Now that he thought about it, his mother had not had time to

get his letter, bake a cherry pie, and send it by mail. Maybe the pie would come later with the sleeping bag. Actually, he now wanted the sleeping bag more than he wanted a cherry pie. The brownies were very fine, especially since they did not have to be shared with Bert Bullock. As usual, he had gone off on one of his mysterious errands to the counselors' hut.

"I'm going because," said Jumbo.

"And just when you've got promoted to Sailfish!" wondered Josh, who was still a Minnow. "But you're leaving because of Red Bull, aren't you, Jumbo?"

"Well, all right, that's why, then," said Jumbo. "I can't stand him and I'm not getting anything to eat and I called up my mother. She's coming to get me tomorrow."

"What did you tell her?" asked Spider.

"I told her I felt sick, and I do."

There seemed to be nothing more to say about it. The four finished the brownies in silence. Then Josh climbed out of his bunk and hid the empty box at the bottom of his locker. You never could be sure what Bert would think was a sin. They all had more than enough holes in their charts, even Boris. It was better to conceal the evidence of the feast.

Whether because of the brownies or because of his feelings about Jumbo's departure, Josh slept uneasily. He dreamed that he was lost in the woods and

that Bert Bullock was chasing him. In the middle of
the night he rolled about and fell out of his bunk,
landing on the floor with a crash that woke up
everybody except Bert. He had come in late and
slept like a log while the others obligingly climbed
out of bed and helped Josh remake his bunk. Josh
was not hurt, but he thought he had never had to do
a more awkward, hopeless job than remaking a top
bunk with sheets and blankets in the middle of the
night. He wondered how soon the sleeping bag
would come from home, if ever.

The next morning, while everyone else was swimming, Jumbo's mother and father arrived at Camp
Buddy, as predicted, and took him home. Josh,
Spider, and Boris felt depressed when they came
back from the lake and saw Jumbo's empty bunk
and shelves. Good old Jumbo! He had left a pile of
comic books on Josh's bunk for a parting present.
Above Jumbo's own bunk was a new message written in black crayon: WHAT A CABIN—HA HA!

Bert Bullock saw it when he arrived a moment
later. "That fat chicken! The Establishment are all
hot and bothered about why he went home. How
would I know? Why would they ask me?" he
snorted. "Step on it, you guys. There's early lunch
today before the Treasure Hunt."

He stepped out of his wet swimming suit, kicked
it under his bunk, and began to pull on his dry

clothes. "Anybody that's late for lunch gets a knuckle rub." With this parting shot he took off at a run.

Josh was kneeling down, fumbling with a shoe-lace. Bert Bullock always made him feel clumsy and slow. Suddenly, out of the corner of his eye he saw Boris on his knees, too, by Bert's bunk. Boris' arm reached under the bunk and pulled out the wet swimming suit. Quickly he zipped open Bert's sleeping bag. Then he dropped the suit into the bag and zipped it closed again.

"There," he said. "A little surprise for Red Bull when he goes to bed tonight. And I'll bet Cabin 13 won't be getting the Skunk again because of that swimming suit."

Josh stared. "But—but what will he do when he finds out?"

"Who cares?" said Boris. "Are you a man or a mouse? Squeak up! Come on, there's the lunch bell."

But Josh did not feel much like eating lunch. For once his small share seemed plenty. Tonight when Bert found his wet swimming suit, there would be knuckle rubs for everybody in Cabin 13! He kept glancing from Spider to Boris and then to Bert, who had jogged three times around the field before lunch to get in shape, he said, and to soften up his football shoes some more. He was now attacking a second

heaping plate of spaghetti. Josh thought Spider looked rather worried, but Boris seemed perfectly unconcerned.

With the arrival of stewed cherries for dessert, Mr. Warden stood up to explain the rules for the Treasure Hunt. As usual, he looked cheerful and kind and rather tired.

"You'll start out right after lunch," he said. "You'll go in pairs and each pair will be given a clue. That will lead you to a second clue. Each clue will tell you where to go next, if you can guess what it means. The clues are hidden all over the woods, down by the lake, and in some of the camp buildings. The first ones are easy, but they get harder as you go along. No one is to go beyond the camp grounds under any circumstances. The winning pair will get ten extra points for their cabin, a badge for each boy, and a special prize which I'll give out tonight after dinner. Counselors will be assigned to make safety checks at special points and will be responsible for seeing that all boys get back in time for dinner. Come up here to the head table by pairs when I call your names and I'll give you your first clue."

Josh and Spider were called up together. Boris was to go with a boy from another cabin. Josh was sorry about that. He would rather have gone with Boris. Spider still seemed to rub Josh the wrong way.

It was like Spider now to snatch the folded piece of paper from Mr. Warden's hand and run from the dining hall before letting Josh see it.

"Wait up!" he called to Spider. All around the dining hall excited pairs of boys were holding whispered consultations as they got their clues and started off in various directions.

On the steps of the dining hall Josh caught up with Spider, who stood puzzling over the piece of paper. " 'Keep it clean,' " Josh read. "What does that mean?"

" 'Keep it clean,' " repeated Spider. "Hey, that's not fair. That doesn't tell us anything."

"Wait a minute," said Josh. "Look at the pictures, too. They must mean something." Under the words were two drawings—a piece of soap, clearly labeled, and a castle.

"That's no help," said Spider.

Josh let out a whoop. "Yes, it is." Then lowering his voice, "Look! Soap and palace. The Soap Palace! Come on!" He wanted to say, "Come on, stupid," but refrained.

Spider looked at Josh with the first admiration he had shown. "Right!" he shouted. "Let's go!"

The two raced off to the end of the path that led between the cabins. The long low Soap Palace stood just beyond, and it was only a moment's work to dash in and begin the search for the second clue.

Josh found it, an envelope marked "Cobb and Spears—Clue 2," fastened with Scotch tape to the container that held paper towels. He tore off the envelope and ripped it open. Inside was a paper with more cryptic words: "Big fish swallow little fish."

Spider grabbed the paper from Josh's hands. "Let's see," he demanded. "Is there a picture?" There was—a picture of the dock with a "stick man" diving off at the deep end.

"Down to the lake," yelled Spider, and they were off again, back along the path between the cabins, passing other pairs of treasure hunters, some running, some puzzling over clues or arguing. Josh and Spider ran down the long gravelly slope to the beach and on to the dock. There was Dusty Moore, cooling his feet in the water as he leaned comfortably against a post. He was plinking on a ukulele and humming to himself.

"Where's the clue?" panted Spider.

"Look around," Dusty said. "Only watch your step."

Josh and Spider went over the dock inch by inch but saw no sign of a clue. From the hill above them came a triumphant shout.

"Darn it," said Spider, stamping his foot. "Some other guys must have won."

"Don't worry," said Dusty. "There are lots of clues. The hunt will take all afternoon. You've got

plenty of time. Keep looking. What did your last clue say?"

"Big fish swallow little fish," Josh told him. He took the clue from Spider's hand and began to study it again.

Dusty laughed. "Big fish? That's a good one." But he would not give them a hint. They heard another shout from the hill, this time near the Crafts Cabin.

Spider sat down on the dock. "What's the use?" he said. "We'll never find this one. We'll be spending the whole afternoon right here."

Suddenly Josh ran to the end of the dock. "Whales are big fish," he called back to Spider. "Here's where the Whales swim." He lay down on his stomach and looked under the edge of the dock. "I've got it!" he yelled. "Here's the clue!"

There was a piece of paper fastened to the wood with a thumbtack. He tore it off and raced back to Spider. Together they examined the paper. The clue read: "Moan! Groan!" With it was a picture of a cabin which looked to Josh like the camp infirmary, known as the Sick Bay, a small building that stood in a clump of trees not far from the Soap Palace. He told Spider his guess.

"No, it's not," said Spider firmly. "That's no infirmary. I know what it is. I remember from the Ghost Hike last year. Follow me!" Tossing his long

61

hair out of his eyes, he tore off up the long slope to the camp with Josh at his heels.

"Don't go off bounds," Dusty called after them. Josh waved to show he had heard, but Spider only ran on.

SEVEN

Good Old Spider

"Spider, are you sure you know where we're going?" asked Josh. They had stopped running a long, long time ago and had been walking single file along a narrow path edged with brambles. Josh did not know what time it was but he knew that he was hungry and tired. They were still in the woods, and had turned away from the lake so that nothing could be seen but pine trees, underbrush that scratched their legs, and the little path which seemed to go on

63

forever under a sky now gray and overcast with clouds.

"Of course I know where we're going," Spider said confidently. "I have a perfect sense of direction. My father says so. I told you twenty times that clue means the haunted house. I went there last year on the Ghost Hike and I remember every step of the way. It's right along here somewhere. We'll come to it in a minute."

"But I think we're outside the camp grounds," Josh said. "When we went through that wire fence about an hour ago, wasn't that the edge of the camp?"

"There are lots of old fences around here," Spider told him. "You just follow me."

They came to a fork in the path. Spider hesitated for a moment, then set off to the left. The path continued to meander through the bushes until it was crossed by a fallen tree. Beyond the tree there was no sign of a path. Spider stopped and scratched his head.

"That's funny," he said. "This tree must have fallen since last year."

"I don't know," said Josh, "but it looks to me as if it's been lying there for about a *hundred* years. Let's sit down and have a rest. And let's look at this clue again." He pulled the paper from his shirt pocket and they sat down on the tree trunk. "I still think that picture looks like the Sick Bay," he argued.

64

"Well, maybe it does," Spider sighed. "If that's the Sick Bay, we've sure come a long way for nothing. And I've never been lost before."

"There's always a first time," said Josh, quoting a favorite saying of his mother. "We'd better be getting back." It was a funny thing but he did not feel mad at Spider for getting lost and getting Josh lost with him. In fact, he liked Spider much better than he had before.

They started running along the path in the direction from which they had come. Once again Spider stopped. "I don't see the path," he said. "It—it just sort of ends in the bushes here."

They began to wander about in the underbrush looking for the path.

"How could it disappear like that?" said Josh. "We came right along it before. It's *got* to be somewhere. Hey, Spider, let's not get separated. You know what I think? I think we're *really* lost now!"

"We can't be *really* lost," Spider told him. "We're not far from camp. You know that."

"Yes," said Josh, "but if we aren't lost, where are we?"

"We'll find out," Spider said. "You know what we ought to do? We ought to climb a tree. Then we can get a look around, before—before it gets dark. Help me find a good tree."

The search for a good tree took time. Colors faded. The darkness closed in.

"Listen, Spider," said Josh. "Did you hear that?"

Spider was clambering up a pine tree. Small branches kept snapping and breaking, but he went on up, higher and higher. He did not answer.

"I thought I heard the dinner bell at camp," Josh called. "I think it came from over that way, to the left. Can you see anything over to the left?"

"Not yet," panted Spider, from above. "I can't see a thing anywhere. Too many branches."

"Maybe you'd better come down," called Josh. "You're getting up awfully high. Maybe those branches aren't very strong."

He heard a loud snap above him and Spider came down. The branches of the pine tree waved wildly as a dark object came hurtling down through them and thudded to the ground. Spider rolled over and lay still at Josh's feet.

"Spider!" Josh cried. "Spider!" He stared aghast at the crumpled figure. Then he began to cry in earnest. Spider must have fallen at least twenty feet. "Help! Help!" he sobbed. "Somebody come! Spider's dead!"

Spider sat up. "I'm not dead," he said. He pushed his long hair out of his eyes. "I guess I'm not dead. Just got knocked out for a minute, that's all. Only, my right arm hurts."

Josh squatted beside him and wiped his eyes on his sleeve. "Gee, Spider," he said. "Good old Spider!

I'm glad you're all right. I thought there for a minute . . . Can you walk? Do you want to just lie
there for a while? Or what?"

"Maybe I can walk," said Spider. "I can try. But I
don't know the way. I'm lost. I'm *so* lost." In the
gathering night Josh heard a sniff.

"Spider," said Josh, "I'm almost sure I heard the
dinner bell somewhere over to the left. It sounded
pretty far away, but we could try. Here, put your
good arm around my shoulder and sort of lean on
me."

He heard another sniff and then Spider's voice
quavered, "My arm hurts too much."

"Look," said Josh, "maybe I can make a sling, like
this." He pulled off his T-shirt, tied the sleeves
together, and slipped the improvised sling over
Spider's head. The body of the shirt supported the
injured arm. It was not easy to adjust the sling in the
dark with Spider moaning and crying, but Josh kept
at it until the job was done.

"Thanks," Spider said faintly. "That feels better.
Maybe I can make it now, if you know where to
go."

He stood up somewhat shakily and put his left
arm around Josh's shoulder. Slowly they started forward, side by side. Trees loomed, threatening, and
brambles snatched at them, but they kept on. Josh
tried to steer a course to the left as well as he could.

A sound echoed through the woods. "Whoo! Whoo! . . . Whoo! Whoo!"

"What's that?" gasped Josh. "Are we near that haunted house?"

Spider managed a weak grin. "That's no ghost. That's the camp siren. They must know we're lost. It *is* over to the left. Let's keep going that way."

On they went, with better heart now, while the friendly siren kept sending out its signals. They stumbled over roots and got well scratched by the brambles, but they never stopped.

"You're doing fine, Spider," Josh told him again and again. "Just keep going. Left, left, left my wife and ninety-nine children at home in bed in starving condition with nothing but gingerbread left, left . . . Come on, you're doing fine." One foot in front of another, on and on through the dark they went.

And all at once they saw lights flashing among the trees. Voices were calling. "Cobb! Spears! Cobb! Where are you? Hello-o-o! Hello-o-o!"

"Here!" shouted Josh. "Here we are! Over here!"

Mr. Warden and half a dozen counselors were running toward them, looking as huge as bears in the night. But Josh could not be scared with the friendly voices calling back and forth, "They're all right! We've found them! Spears has hurt his arm. Make a chair."

Spider was being carried between two counselors.

69

Dusty Moore was patting Josh on the shoulder and saying, "Good work, Cobb." And at long last the lights of camp were twinkling in the distance. A few more minutes brought them to the path between the cabins and a crowd of boys running out to meet them, full of cheers and questions.

While Spider's arm was being examined and put in a splint, Josh was given all the supper he could eat and sent to bed early. Spider would spend the night in the Sick Bay, with the nurse to look after him. Boris turned in early, too. He wanted to hear about Josh's adventure in the woods.

"Who won the Treasure Hunt?" asked Josh, as they settled down in their bunks.

"We never heard," Boris told him. "Hunting for you and Spider was the main thing. What happened?"

Josh told the whole story and then asked "Where's Bert?"

"Who knows?" said Boris. "He didn't turn up for supper at all, and no one has seen him since then. Mr. Warden's awful mad. Old Red Bull was supposed to be on duty somewhere on the camp boundary line this afternoon, and if he wasn't where he was supposed to be, maybe that's why you got lost, Mr. Warden said."

They went on talking comfortably and happily, accompanied by the cricket and frog orchestra, until

70

almost midnight, when Josh whispered, "Shh! Someone's coming!" The screen door creaked open and
the dark figure of Bert Bullock slipped quietly into
Cabin 13, undressed, and slid into his sleeping bag.
Josh and Boris smiled in the dark as they saw him
leap out again. They watched with satisfaction while
he fished out the wet swimming suit, shivering and
muttering. It was good to know that Mr. Bert Bullock would spend a restless night in the damp in-
terior of that bag. As for knuckle rubs, there would
be time enough tomorrow to worry about that. Josh
and Boris closed their eyes and slept the sleep of the
just.

EIGHT

The Establishment Takes Control

Later that night it began to rain, and it was still pouring the next morning. Bert slept so soundly that Josh and Boris had left the cabin when he woke. He was the last one into the dining hall for breakfast. That was why Bert was the only person in camp who was surprised when Mr. Warden left the head table and crossed the room in what looked like about three giant steps.

Bert had only had time to growl, "Where's

73

Spider?" when Mr. Warden was standing over him and saying in a low voice, "See me in my office immediately after breakfast, Bullock."

Everyone stopped talking and watched with awe while Mr. Warden returned to the head table and sat down, looking grim. The Establishment might be the last to find out when something went wrong, but when it did find out, it was formidable. Josh and Boris kept their heads down and applied themselves to eating their cereal.

Bert looked unconcerned. He bit into a roll, chewed it for a long time, as if it had turned into sawdust, and stared nonchalantly around the room. No one met his eyes. He shrugged, raised his eyebrows, yawned, stretched, and suddenly left the table. As the screen door swung closed behind him, a subdued hum of conversation began again with an undercurrent of excited speculation.

"I guess he still doesn't know what happened to you and Spider last night," said Boris. "I wish I could hear what Mr. Warden says when he tells old Red Bull about it."

"But where do you suppose he was all that time?" Josh wondered again. "And what's going to happen to him?"

"Plenty, I'll bet," said Boris.

Mr. Warden departed for his office soon afterward and the head counselor made the announcements

for the Establishment. Saturday night there would be a campfire with singing and skits. If you wanted to be in a skit, you should meet Dusty Moore right after breakfast. There would be a church service on Sunday morning. White shirts and ties were required.

Because of the rain, there would be no outdoor sports. Campers could play ping-pong or shuffleboard on the porch of the dining hall. The Crafts Cabin was open for anyone who wanted to make things. The camp library, also in the Crafts Cabin, had plenty of good books. Everyone who wanted to could write something for the camp paper, *The Camp Buddy Breeze*. It could be news, a story, a poem, or a joke—anything you wanted to write. All campers were urged to contribute. Cheers and groans. The candy counter would be open for an hour after lunch. Cheers. One candy bar per camper was the limit that could be bought. Groans.

They would probably all like to know about David Spears. The nurse was driving him into the town hospital to see the doctor. They would know by lunchtime whether Spears could come back to camp or whether he would have to be sent home. Everyone should be careful not to go beyond the camp boundaries, which were clearly marked by the wire fences. And no one was to climb trees. Until the rain stopped, any camper seen outdoors without

poncho and rubbers would get a hole in his chart. Any questions?

There were many questions, which the head counselor answered patiently until signs of disorder appeared. Paper napkins, wadded up, were being flipped and thrown. Plates were skidding across tables or being piled high with reckless abandon. The counselors looked gloomy. A rainy day at camp was a test of character for counselors.

At last the campers were dismissed from the dining hall and scattered according to their choices.

"What are you going to do?" asked Boris.

"Get my poncho and rubbers first, I guess," said Josh. "Then maybe I'll see if I can be in a skit."

In his usual well-organized way, Boris had his poncho and rubbers, but he said, "I'll go back to the cabin with you . . . Gee! Jumbo's gone. Spider's gone. There's nobody left in our cabin but you and me. I don't want to be in a skit. I can't do that kind of stuff. Why don't we do something together the rest of the morning?"

"Yes, let's," Josh said. "But you could be in a skit, Boris. I know one we did in school. It's about Superman and the little tiny ninety-seven-pound weakling. It's pretty good."

Boris looked doubtful but said he would think about it. They reached Cabin 13 and ran in out of the rain. Then they stopped short. Bert Bullock was standing by his bunk, packing his duffel bag. They

looked at him silently. The rain drummed on the roof. After a quick glance at the boys, Bert continued to pack without explanations. He wrapped his football shoes tenderly in his pajamas and fitted them into the top of the duffel bag with loving care.

Josh searched through his trunk for his poncho and rubbers. Boris sat down on his own bunk and began to turn the pages of a comic book. At last he said, "Where—where are you going?"

"To get a job in town," Bert answered shortly. "I'm through with this crummy camp."

Josh pulled his rubbers over his wet sneakers. "Who will be our counselor?" he asked.

"How should I know?" answered Bert. "Some poor jerk. And then you can complain about *him* and Warden can chew him out."

"Complain?" Boris said indignantly. "We never complained. We never said a word."

"If that's true," said Bert. "Which I doubt."

He heaved his duffel bag to his shoulder and picked up his suitcase. Josh ran to the door and held it open.

"I get the idea," Bert said. "If I didn't have my hands full, you'd get a knuckle rub."

"I was only trying to help," Josh told him. Bert marched out into the rain and disappeared. Josh gave a sigh of relief and said, "Come on. Let's go and find Dusty."

Dusty, as it turned out, had taken over one end of

the deserted dining hall and had gathered around him all the would-be performers for Saturday night's campfire skits. As Boris and Josh arrived, he was saying, "Now we need a barbershop quartet for the 'Chocolate Pie Song.' " There was laughter. All the old campers remembered the "Chocolate Pie Song" from the year before and several boys made a disorganized try at words or music or both.

Dusty nodded when he saw the two newcomers. "Cobb and Morris! Good! Have you got a skit?"

"Not yet," Josh said, "but we could do one if we had another guy with us. He shouldn't be very big."

Dusty looked around the group of campers. "How about Kippy?" he asked. He pointed to a small boy and Josh saw that it was the little baseball player, the same one who had sprinted past him in the track meet. "Kippy Dawes," Dusty said in explanation. "Kip, why don't you get together somewhere with Josh and Boris and see what you can work out?"

He turned to them again as he picked up his ukulele. "By the way, Mr. Warden has just told me that I'm moving into Cabin 13 with part of my crew. We had to split up and move because our cabin has sprung a bad leak in the roof. Kippy is coming with me and so is Chatty Lucas. You'll meet him later if you don't already know him. He wrote the 'Chocolate Pie Song.' "

"Come on, then," said Josh, looking at Boris and

Kippy. "Let's go back to the cabin. We don't want everybody to see our skit till it's ready." In great good humor the three paddled off toward Cabin 13, while Dusty continued his search as a talent scout for a quartet to sing the "Chocolate Pie Song."

When he had led the way into Cabin 13, Josh insisted on rolling down the awnings for privacy. Boris pointed out that this should have been done earlier. The floor at the front of the cabin was soaking wet and the lower bunks were none too dry. That was one good thing about being in a top bunk, Josh thought. Everything had its bright side!

It was cozy and pleasant with the awnings down. Josh explained the skit. He would be the tiny weakling. He would stand behind a table with sneakers on his hands, so he would look very short. Kippy would stand behind Josh with his arms under Josh's shoulders like the arms of the tiny weakling. Then Superman would come in. That would be Boris. They could figure out the costumes later, and Josh would try to remember the words they had used in the skit at school, or maybe make up some new ones.

Boris decided he did not mind being Superman. Kippy was willing to be the weakling's arms, if Josh would show him what to do. And Josh did not mind being in charge. The morning passed happily.

About noon, Dusty Moore appeared, with Chatty Lucas trailing him. Josh remembered he had heard

someone say that Chatty was very funny. But he was silent most of the time, spent hours in the camp library whenever he could, and seldom if ever smiled. Josh wondered how a person like that could be funny. Chatty said he would rather not be in the skit, but he would help with the costumes and the props.

The rain had stopped. Dusty pulled up the awnings on a world of green, drenched with golden sunshine. Then he set about the job of moving in. Everyone helped, and Cabin 13 was shipshape in no time at all. As they stowed away the last items, Josh finally asked what everyone was bursting to know. "Dusty, where was Bert last night?"

"I guess it's no secret," Dusty answered. "All the counselors know. Bert has a girl in the town where he lives. It's about fifty miles from here. He's been calling her up every day and and every night. He was always up at the counselors' hut, telephoning."

Boris and Josh exchanged looks. So! That mystery was solved.

"But last night?" prodded Boris.

"Well, it seems she asked Bert why he didn't hitch a ride home so they could have a date . . . and he did."

"We're glad he's gone," Boris said. That closed the subject. Neither Boris nor Josh ever mentioned the knuckle rubs or the towel snapping.

"I almost forgot," Dusty said. "The mail was in just before we came. Josh, there's a package for you at the counselors' hut. It's awfully big, but not heavy. Do you want to get it now?"

When Josh opened the package a few minutes later, his happiness was complete. It was a brand-new sleeping bag.

NINE

Buddy Shines

The following days made Cabin 13 seem like a different place.

Kippy and Chatty were great guys, Josh thought. Kippy made up for his small size with enough will power and energy for two boys, and Chatty, who was so silent in a crowd, could talk well enough when there were only two or three around. He did not like to argue, though. He said arguing "just stirred up a lot of bug dust." Chatty really was a funny guy.

Of course the biggest difference in Cabin 13 was having Dusty instead of Bert Bullock for a counselor. Bert had always seemed to be the enemy. Dusty was on your side. He still had to put a hole in your chart if you were not on time, or if you and your possessions were not clean and neat. But it did not give Dusty any pleasure to do it. Looking back, it seemed to the boys that Bert had enjoyed jabbing his pencil through the charts. That was a very big difference.

Everyone was getting enough to eat now, too. Dusty served out the food, "even Stephen," Chatty said. (He and Kippy were horrified when they heard about the starvation diet under Bert's regime.) The kitchen would send second helpings on request, if you asked in time. Dusty always asked in time, "so you don't feel like Oliver Twist," as Chatty put it. The other boys just looked at him. He explained how Oliver Twist had to get up enough nerve to ask for more food when he lived at the workhouse. Josh was impressed. This was what came of Chatty's spending all that time in the library. Josh determined to look for *Oliver Twist* the next time he was in the Crafts Cabin. Meanwhile, Josh and Boris shoveled in so much food that Cabin 13 got the Pig twice in a row for bad table manners.

Another thing about Dusty was that he always did as much or more than he asked the boys to do. He

himself was not naturally neat, he said, and he thought it was hard to be on time, but he could not ask them to try if he did not try, too.

They began to sing a lot. Dusty taught them to sing a round. They sang it first as a two-part round, then in three parts, then in four, over and over while they cleaned the cabin for inspection, until the campers nearby urged them to pipe down. But Cabin 13 never wanted to pipe down. They sang:

My paddle's keen and bright, flashing with silver,
Follow the wild-goose flight, dip, dip, and swing;
Dip, dip, and swing it back, flashing with silver,
Follow the wild-goose track, dip, dip, and swing.

There was really a new spirit in Cabin 13. They had not yet won the Eagle, but they had stopped getting the Skunk.

Josh did not feel afraid around Dusty. He knew there would never be a knuckle rub from Dusty or the snapping of a towel on sunburned skin. The boys liked to rough-house with Dusty. They knew he was strong enough to hurt them if he wanted to, but he never wanted to hurt.

He was always available if you needed help. He did not help you unless you asked, and sometimes, even if you did ask for help, he only stood by and gave advice, but that was help, too. And Dusty made

no long-winded telephone calls in the counselors' hut when he was meant to be on duty. In fact, he made no telephone calls of any kind and he never received any, so far as Josh knew. He was just always nice and always on the job. That was all that Josh or anyone else in Cabin 13 knew about Dusty.

When Taps sounded and lights went out all over camp, Dusty would lie in his bunk, leaning on one elbow and holding a flashlight on the pages of a book. He had been reading it aloud every night since camp started, and Chatty brought Josh and Boris up to date on the plot.

"Sherlock Holmes and Dr. Watson are out on this moor in England. It's always at night and there's a lot of fog and wind blowing all the time. There's this spooky old house where you can hear something howling out on the moors. And Sherlock Holmes and Dr. Watson are going to find out what it is. It's a neat book."

It *was* a neat book. It was called *The Hound of the Baskervilles*. While Dusty was reading, Josh could feel the wind blowing and see the fog rising around the old house on the moors. His scalp prickled as he started off each night with Sherlock Holmes and Dr. Watson to discover the source of the nameless dread in the lonely dark. And all the time, he was safe and snug in the new sleeping bag in good old Cabin 13. It was great. He could not wait from

Buddy will shine tonight, Buddy will shine!
Buddy will shine tonight, all down the line.
Buddy will shine tonight, Buddy will shine!
When the sun goes down and the moon comes up,
Buddy will shine!

After a while the fire died down to the right size
for a campfire. Then there were skits and more songs
and the moon did come up. It rose from behind the
trees, first huge and golden, then shining brighter
and brighter as it crossed the sky. The man in the
moon looked down at them. Josh could see him
perfectly.

Cabin 13 began "The Canoe Song" and sang it
over and over until all the new boys joined in with
everyone else and sang it as if they would never stop.
Josh thought for the hundredth time of how it must
feel to cross the lake by canoe and wondered if he
would ever swim well enough to earn that honor.

My paddle's keen and bright,
Flashing with silver;
Follow the wild-goose flight,
Dip, dip, and swing.

Finally the time came for Josh's skit. Under cover
of a long song with a lot of verses, Boris and Kippy
helped to set up a card table at one side of the circle
where everybody could see. Josh stood in back of the
card table. His head stuck out above a big cape made

baseball, or to sit on the dock while everyone else went swimming. It was especially tough for Spider, the big athlete. But at least he stopped bragging about how good he was at sports and, instead, gave Josh some special coaching. Maybe it would have happened without Spider's coaching, but Josh graduated from the Tank at the end of the week and became a Sailfish.

Saturday night was fine and clear. The counselors had been busy near the flagpole most of the afternoon, building logs and branches into a great tepee-shaped pile. The senior campers helped by carrying benches from the dining hall after supper to make a double circle around the pile. Long before dark, every seat was filled. Then Mr. Warden stepped into the circle with the head counselor. They lighted torches and thrust them into the woodpile. Almost at once, smoke and flames began to pour out through the branches until the whole pile was one enormous furnace. The camp cheered, and Kenny, the swimming counselor, stood up, raising his arms.

"Buddy Will Shine!" he called. He began to sing and all around the circle, voices joined in. It was such an easy song that everyone could sing it after one try. When they sang it again, a few of the counselors put in some harmony and everyone was belting it out at the top of his lungs:

one night to the next to hear another chapter of *The Hound of the Baskervilles.*

Then Spider came back, with his arm in a plaster cast. That was a red-letter day! Spider said his stay at the hospital wasn't long, but it seemed long.

"Is your arm broken?" Josh asked.

"Oh yes, it's broken, all right," Spider said. "Mr. Warden called my family and he couldn't get them at first. They went away on a trip when I came to camp, so Mr. Warden couldn't send me home. And finally he got them, somewhere in Texas, and I talked to my dad. He said they'd come back and take me home, but I said I didn't want to because Mr. Warden said I could stay at camp."

"But what can you do with your arm in a cast?" asked Boris.

"He can't do much," Dusty said cheerfully. "He can't swim or play baseball or tennis or be in the track meet. But he can eat and sleep and read. He can go to the campfire Saturday night. Maybe he can even go on the overnight hike next week with Mr. Warden and the supplies in the station wagon. And you guys can help me see that Spider gets along all right."

Everybody tried to help Spider. He could not tie his shoes or manage buttons or cut meat, and he had to sit on the sidelines while everyone else played

from one of his blankets. His hands were in a pair of sneakers. They came out from the cape and danced around on the table. The card table was covered with one of Josh's sheets, which hung down all around so that you could not see his real feet on the ground. Someone else was underneath the blanket too. That was Kippy, standing close behind Josh. You could not see him at all, except for his arms, which stuck out from under Josh's shoulders. Kippy's hands waved, scratched Josh's head, covered Josh's mouth when he yawned, pulled out a handkerchief when Josh sneezed. And all the while, Josh was explaining about how terrible it was to be such a tiny little weakling.

Then, Shezam! Boris leaped out of the darkness, dressed as Superman in a tight pair of shorts and another of Josh's sheets for a cape. A big red *S* was painted on his bare chest. He gave the tiny weakling some exercises to do—that was the funniest part—and suddenly, Shezam! Josh came out from behind the table, shedding his blanket and flexing his muscles and standing as tall as Superman, with a big *S* on his own chest. Kippy was left crouching under the blanket to be gathered up later and hurried away with the card table and the other props at the end of the skit.

There was much applause and laughter. Josh and Kippy and Boris had to come back and take a bow.

"And now," announced Kenny, "the 'Chocolate Pie Song,' words and music by Chatty Lucas, as sung by the Camp Buddy Barbershop Quartet, accompanied by Dusty Moore and his orchestra."

Dusty stepped into the circle, tuning his ukulele. A cheer went up. Josh, Boris, and Kippy found their places on the bench with Spider and Chatty, as Dusty's quartet began to sing:

There hasn't been a letter for me
In three times three days' mails,
And I just got seven holes in my chart
For the length of my fingernails,
And yet I can laugh all this away;
Do you ask the reason why?
Just look at me;
It's easy to see
Today we had chocolate pie!

And so whenever the skies are gray
And everything's going wrong,
You'll find it a wonderful help to sing
The Camp Buddy pastry song.
Let others be sour and sad and glum,
Let others groan and sigh;
But why do I grin?
I'm full to the chin—
Today we had chocolate pie!

The second time through, everyone joined in the last lines, rubbing their stomachs. The third time,

Dusty led the quartet in a buck-and-wing, playing the ukulele as he led the dance around the circle, while they hummed and whistled and clapped. Then Dusty called, "Chatty, take a bow." Silent as ever, Chatty stood up and sat down again. Everyone thought the "Chocolate Pie Song" was a work of genius. Josh thought it was the best thing he had ever heard in his whole life. Dusty made Chatty take another bow.

Josh's heart swelled. Good old Dusty, the best counselor in camp! The greatest guy in the whole world! Somehow, before the end of camp he would like to do something to make Dusty proud that he, Josh, was in Cabin 13.

You could not get into the dining hall at all on Sunday nights at Camp Buddy unless you had written home. Josh's letter said, "Dear Mother: We had a campfire last night. Our cabin did a skit. It was pretty good. It was lucky you sent those sheets and blankets. You don't need to send the cherry pie after all. Today we had chocolate pie. Love, Josh."

TEN

Dusty Trail

The overnight hike followed a trail of about five miles, ending at a good camping site across the lake from Camp Buddy. Each day of the second week at camp, the boys from two cabins set off together with their counselors. Mr. Warden followed later, bringing cooking utensils, food, and emergency supplies by station wagon along a dirt road that circled the lake. The campers did not follow the road. The narrow trail, up hill and down,

was more exciting. There were times when it was almost like mountain climbing. At night, the boys who had not yet made the overnight hike could see the campfires on the shore across the lake and longed for their turn. Those who had made the hike said that it was the most fun of anything at camp.

When Mr. Warden announced that Cabin 5 and Cabin 13 would hike the next day, Dusty explained what must be done.

"You'll carry your ponchos and sleeping bags in a harness on your back. Put your toothbrush, soap, towel, and swimming suit inside your roll. I'll show you how to tie it firm and tight. You want to have your hands free for a little rock scrambling. If the weather is good, we'll have a swim before supper. At night we make a shelter out of the ponchos in case of rain. Got it?"

They all got it. But rolling up his sleeping bag was not as simple as it had sounded to Josh. If he lashed it tight at one side, it spilled out of its moorings at the other side. He was still struggling with it long after Boris had made a neat roll of his sleeping bag and gone off to collect leather harnesses for Dusty, Kippy, Chatty, Josh, and himself. Spider would not need a harness. He would ride to the camp site in the station wagon with Mr. Warden.

Josh envied Spider. He could see now that there were some advantages in every situation, even in

having a broken arm. If he, Josh, had a broken arm, Dusty would be making up a pack for him, competently and quickly, as he was doing for Spider. Dusty offered to help Josh, but without a broken arm, Josh was too proud to accept help. Dusty went off at a trot to stow Spider's pack in the station wagon. Then Boris returned with the harnesses. They helped one another to shoulder their loads.

Before Dusty returned, a whistle blew to signal that Cabin 5 and Cabin 13 should assemble at the starting point on the porch of the dining hall. Dusty shouldered his pack quickly and there was no time for Josh to make further improvements on his own pack. He knew at once, from the feel of it on his back, that it was going to be awkward and uneven every step of the way.

Then they were off, Cabin 5 leading the way with Kenny at the head of the column. Cabin 13 followed, Dusty bringing up the rear. Kenny was a good pace-setter, not too fast, not too slow. The column snaked along the dusty path under the pine trees. After a while someone began to sing:

> Over hill, over dale, as we hit the dusty trail
> And the caissons go rolling along . . .

Josh kept his eyes on the path, but his view included Boris' legs moving steadily, just ahead of

him. Behind, he heard the soft thud of Chatty's sneakers, and behind that, Kippy's quicker steps. Kippy's legs were short, but he would never be a straggler if he could help it. Dusty was whistling.

Now and then Josh hunched his shoulders to make his unwieldy pack ride more comfortably. He recognized part of the path where he and Spider had got lost. They came to a wire fence, followed it to a five-barred gate, and were outside the grounds of Camp Buddy.

The path began to climb beside a little stream that sparkled and trickled over its stony bed from some hidden spring in the hillside.

"Take a breather," called Kenny. The column halted and the boys looked back over the path along which they had come. The sun was still hot and high. A carpet of pine needles underfoot sent up a spicy smell. Above and below the steep slope, the pine boughs whispered and sighed. For a moment the hikers listened to the silence. Then someone said, "Gee!" Someone else laughed, and the column started forward again.

They skirted a pasture where cows were grazing and passed a farmer's house. A smell of fresh baking came from the open kitchen window. Josh remembered that another long letter had arrived from his mother. He must take time to read it all the way through when he got back to camp. But why did his

mother write such long letters? He forgot her again as the lake appeared once more below them. They clambered down to the beach and stopped again. Now they could see the lake as they had never seen it from Camp Buddy. Little waves glinted in the late afternoon sunlight. The dark pines marched down to the edge of the water from the surrounding hills, and far off across the lake a thin thread of blue smoke rose from a chimney among treetops.

They had spotted Camp Buddy itself and could see how far they had come. A canoe heading for the distant dock was a tiny red dash with two dots above it. Then two far-away oars flashed in the sunlight. "Dip, dip, and swing it back," Josh thought. Some day he would swim well enough, and he would win the right to paddle a canoe. He knew now that that day would surely come.

The last part of the hike followed the lake shore. Suddenly there was a sandy stretch of beach before them, with two circles of stones enclosing the charred sticks of old campfires. And there was the station wagon, bumping along a dirt road through the woods. It came to a halt and Mr. Warden waved to the approaching hikers as he climbed out of the big car and began to unpack supplies. Spider climbed out after him. When the station wagon was unpacked, there would be room in the back of it for Mr. Warden and Spider and their sleeping bags.

Kenny and Dusty made everyone help before they could think of a swim. Mr. Warden let them make camp and build fires by themselves, so there was plenty for everyone to do. Josh slid out of his harness and gave a sigh of relief as he let his bedroll drop to the ground.

"Bedrolls up here," Dusty called from the edge of the woods. Josh lugged his burden to the spot pointed out and unrolled it.

"First we'll set up our shelter," said Dusty. "Ponchos over here."

Josh stared at his unrolled sleeping bag. In the center of it lay a toothbrush, a cake of soap, a towel, and a swimming suit. "I forgot my poncho," he said.

So they were minus one poncho when they made the shelter for Cabin 13. Cord was threaded through the eyelets at the edges of the other ponchos, and a sizable rubber roof was the result. Stout wooden stakes, brought by Mr. Warden, were pounded into the earth and the roof was tied firmly to the stakes. It would be easy to crawl into the sleeping bags that were laid out under the poncho roof.

"But not my bag," said Josh. "I don't need to be under the shelter. I don't want to."

"Come on," Boris said. "There's plenty of room."

But Josh refused. He was ashamed to be the only one without a poncho and he thought that every

other boy would hate him if he squeezed in under, anyway.

The swim before supper was fun. It helped him forget his embarrassment, especially since nobody else seemed to be giving even a second thought to his stupidity. Boris showed him how to float on his back, and there he was, able to lie in the water, looking straight up into the evening sky. For one moment, the water and the sky seemed to be the same thing, all one, above and below him. It was a queer, scary, but wonderful feeling.

Then Kenny was blowing his whistle and they were all scrambling out of the water to dress around the campfires which the counselors had started. There was a little chill in the air now. Josh felt ravenous. He stood close to the fire, warming himself and turning a hot dog on a stick. There were buns for the wieners, and baked beans were being heated in their own cans. Mr. Warden had brought a big watermelon, and each cabin had a bag of marshmallows to be toasted after supper.

The first star appeared. A waning moon hung above the lake, but the campers did not linger to admire the view. Suddenly everyone was bone-tired. Before it was really dark, there was a general move toward bed.

Josh had found a good place for his sleeping bag under a pine tree where the ground was perfectly

smooth. He could look up through the branches and see the stars. He took one last look at the two poncho shelters. Someone from under the Cabin 5 shelter complained, "I'm lying on a sharp stone." Someone else said, "Shut up." Josh closed his eyes—and at once discovered a spot where the ground under him was far from smooth. There seemed to be something the size of a log under the small of his back. He turned on his side. A stone nudged his ribs. Why, this spot he had picked out was nothing but humps and hollows! But he was too tired to fight it. He turned again and sleep covered him like a wave.

When he woke, his face was wet. He opened his eyes. It was still pitch dark and a fine drizzle of rain was falling. He turned on his side and pulled the hood of his sleeping bag around his face. The rain began to patter on the ground. It made little popping noises on his sleeping bag as the drops got bigger. Josh snuggled down into the depths of his bag.

Then the heavens descended. The rain fell in solid sheets. Josh sat up. The beam of a flashlight shone out from under the poncho shelter of Cabin 13. It made a broad road straight from Josh to the shelter and Dusty's voice was calling, "Josh! Over here! Hurry!"

Josh stood up in his sleeping bag. "I can't run!" he shouted back.

"Then hop!" Dusty called again. And Josh hopped. Like a monkey on a pogo stick he hopped in his sleeping bag, splashing through puddles, slipping, falling, up again, and on through the downpour until he reached the shelter and wormed his way under. He was glad he had been in plenty of sack races or he would never have made it to the shelter. His bag was a mess, but inside it he was dry.

Everyone was awake under the shelter now, moving over to make room for Josh. Dusty was at one end, then Kippy, Chatty, and Boris. Josh moved in beside Boris. Dusty rolled farther toward the edge of the shelter to make more room for the others. His long legs hit a wooden stake, knocking it loose, and a pool of water poured from the sheltering roof all over his sleeping bag. Dusty raised himself on one elbow, reset the wooden stake as well as he could, and fumbled in the dark to attach the poncho to it. Then he settled down again.

Presently the rain stopped. At the edge of the woods the headlights of the station wagon were turned on and a flashlight came bobbing toward the two shelters. It was Mr. Warden, checking. "Everyone all right here? Moore, everyone all right under your shelter?"

"Yes, sir," said Dusty. "Everyone all right here."

Josh lay still. Everyone was *not* all right. Dusty had had about a bucketful of rain dumped right on

top of him and it was all Josh's fault. No one slept much for the rest of the night. Josh could have sworn he hadn't slept a wink. He seemed only to have closed his eyes for a moment and opened them to see the sun beginning to burn through the mist on the lake.

In the morning the troubles of the night were forgotten. The ground had dried quickly. Mr. Warden produced enough dry wood from the station wagon to start a campfire, and bacon and eggs on paper plates made the campers feel like kings.

"Strike camp!" was the next order. By nine o'clock they had hit the trail. They returned to Camp Buddy as they had left, in single file, Kenny leading, Dusty bringing up the rear. There were only two differences. Josh carried his muddy sleeping bag in his arms all the way. He had lost his harness somehow during the night. Dusty Moore kept sneezing and sounded hoarse. When they reached Camp Buddy, he reported to the nurse that he had a sore throat. At lunchtime Mr. Warden told Cabin 13 that Dusty was in the infirmary.

ELEVEN

The Cheese Stands Alone

Two days later Dusty was still in Sick Bay but his temperature was normal. A steady stream of counselors and campers had been going to see him from the moment when permission was given. The nurse told the boys in Cabin 13 that they could go to see him one at a time. Josh got permission to go in the afternoon while everyone else was playing baseball. He was still on the scrub team and no one seemed to think that it would spoil the game if he was not there.

Dusty was sitting propped up against pillows on a cot that stood against one wall of the little cabin. His ukulele and some books lay on a table at his side.

"Glad to see you. Sit down," he said to Josh, indicating a wooden chair at the foot of the cot. Josh sat down and wrapped his feet around the legs of the chair. He looked at Dusty's face, pale and gaunt in the half light of the cabin.

"I'm sorry you're sick," he blurted out. "It's my fault."

"Your fault?" Dusty echoed. "Why so?"

"Because I forgot my poncho," Josh said, surprised that he should have to explain. Surely Dusty knew? "If I hadn't forgotten my poncho, everybody wouldn't have had to move over and let me in out of the rain. If you hadn't moved over, you wouldn't have got wet and you wouldn't be sick."

Dusty managed a weak smile. "Cobb, you're a worry wart. I probably had a cold coming on, anyway."

"But nobody else forgot his poncho," Josh argued. "I do things like that all the time."

Dusty thought for a moment, appraising Josh with his eyes. "Does your mother do a lot for you at home?" he asked.

Josh nodded. "She says so. I guess she does."

"You get used to having someone remember things for you," Dusty said. "But don't blame her. You're lucky to have a mother. What about your father?"

"He's dead," said Josh. "I don't even remember him."

"I don't remember my father either," Dusty said. "*Or* my mother."

Josh stared. "Not either of them?"

"Not either of them. My father died when I was a baby and my mother married someone else. She thought he wanted me, but he didn't. So she had to

109

put me in The Anchorage. It's an orphanage, really, but it's a good place. She hoped we could be together again some time. At least, that's what they told me at The Anchorage. But I haven't heard from her for years. For a while letters came from different places, but then they stopped."

Josh burned with a sense of outrage and sorrow. "You never had any home at all?"

"Oh, I wouldn't say that." Dusty's voice was matter-of-fact. "I was in a couple of foster homes most of the time, and they were great—one of them, especially. The Anchorage found them for me. Then Mr. Warden came on the board of directors of The Anchorage and he asked if I'd like to be a counselor here at camp. I've been a counselor for three years now and I like it better than anything I've ever done. I lived at The Anchorage last winter and went to school."

"Why did you leave your foster homes if you liked them so much?" Josh asked, frowning with dismay.

"Different reasons. The first one was sold and my foster parents had to move to a little apartment. My second foster father had a chance to go into business in another state and the law said I couldn't live in any other state until I was eighteen."

"But why didn't someone adopt you?" cried Josh. The impact of Dusty's story disturbed him to his bone marrow.

110

"Because my mother might come back," Dusty explained. "For a long while I wished I could be adopted and really belong to someone. But it doesn't matter now."

"How do you mean, it doesn't matter?"

"I'm eighteen now. I've graduated from high school and I'm going into the Marine Corps as soon as camp is over."

Josh was silent. He sat looking at Dusty in awe mingled with disbelief. How could Dusty even talk about such a lonely life? And now, the Marine Corps!

"Does it sound bad to you?" asked Dusty, guessing Josh's thought. He sat up straighter, clasping his bent knees. "Well, you're wrong. It's not bad. A lot of men have been father to me and at least two women have been mother—my two foster mothers."

"And brothers," Josh said hesitantly. "I guess you've got lots of brothers—here at camp, I mean." Suddenly he had an inspiration. "Dusty, don't go into the Marine Corps. Come and live at my house. We've got lots of room."

Dusty laughed softly and shook his head. "Thanks, Josh," he said. "That sounds great. But I know what I'm doing. First off, I want to do my military service now. The service is home for a lot of guys who haven't any other. Then, you see, I can save my pay and go to college."

Josh made one last try. "We really need a man in our family."

"Sure you do," Dusty said. "And you're it."

"Me?" said Josh. "I'm only ten."

"That doesn't matter," Dusty told him. "You can be a man."

Again Josh was silent, his head whirling with new thoughts, his feelings deeply stirred.

"Don't be afraid of anything," Dusty went on. "You can take what comes." He paused. "I'll tell you something. When I was little, living in my first foster home, all the kids in the neighborhood used to play 'Farmer's in the Dell.' The way we played it, when the 'cheese' was chosen, he had to stand alone in the middle of the circle. Remember . . . 'The cheese stands alone'? If I was the cheese, I was scared to death. Everyone in the circle would sing, 'We all pound the cheese' and then they would run in and hit me. Not very hard, but I was always afraid it was going to hurt."

"I know," said Josh. "That's how we played it, too, and I felt just the same."

"So I didn't want to play at all," Dusty said. "I used to cry and run in the house when they started playing that game."

"So did I," said Josh, in a wondering tone. "But I got over it."

"That's what happens," Dusty assured him. "You

112

get over it. You find out that the game is nothing to be scared of. It's even fun. You find that out all along the way. And the sooner you have to take care of yourself, the sooner you start enjoying whatever comes. It's hard to explain. It's just a sort of feeling you have about yourself—but it makes all the difference. Sometimes your first summer at camp can be the start of feeling right about yourself." He paused. "You were afraid of Bert Bullock, weren't you?"

Josh nodded. "We all were."

"He was bad news," Dusty said. "The kind who can spoil camp, especially for a new boy. But even while he was here, you still had some good times, didn't you?"

"Sure we did," said Josh, grinning. "It wasn't all bad, even then. I wish Jumbo hadn't left. He should have stuck it out."

"Why don't you write to him?" Dusty said. "I'll get you his address. He might want to come back. Tell him his bunk is waiting."

"Dusty," Josh asked suddenly, "do you think you'll ever get married?" As soon as he had said it, he turned red and wished he hadn't. But Dusty did not laugh or seem to mind it.

"I've thought about it," he said. "I hope I will some day. But I've got to get through college first. I'll be practically an old man."

The nurse appeared in the doorway, looking at

her watch. "Time's up," she said, in her no-nonsense tone.

"Just a minute," Josh begged. "I have to ask one more thing."

She was merciful and went away, giving permission for one more minute.

"Dusty," Josh asked, "are you going to be well in time for the track meet tomorrow?"

"I doubt it," Dusty said. "You'll all have to get along the best you can. I'll give you a few pointers, if you think you can remember."

"I'll remember," Josh promised.

"Then, tie your shoelaces in a double knot. Keep your eyes straight ahead. Don't look from side to side to see how anyone else is doing. Keep running full speed right up to, and past, the tape. Don't slow down till the race is over. And run every race to win."

He picked up his ukulele as Josh started out the door. Dusty seemed to be feeling a lot better. Josh was feeling better, too.

TWELVE

The Die-Hards

Before suppertime Josh wrote two letters. The first said only, "Dear Jumbo: Why don't you come back? Camp is great now. Red is gone. Dusty Moore is our counselor. He is an orphan. Six guys have shaved their heads bald. Spider did. You have to have permission from home if you want to do it. Chatty and Kippy are in our cabin, but your bunk is still empty. Your friend, Josh."

The second letter said, "Dear Mother: Can I stay

for two more weeks at camp? All the other guys in our cabin are staying. Maybe Jumbo is coming back. Our counselor is Dusty Moore. He is an orphan. After camp he will be in the Marine Corps. Can he come and stay at our house first? Can he come for Christmas? Can he live with us after the Marine Corps? You would like to take care of him. He is on time and neat and everything. I will ask him tomorrow. Love, Josh. P.S. Thanks for the letter. It was very interesting. P.P.S. Can I shave my head?"

Mr. Warden appeared at Lights Out to see if everything was under control in Cabin 13. He said that Dusty would be out of Sick Bay in time for the banquet after the track meet.

"But not in time for the track meet?" asked Josh.

"Probably not, especially if it's a hot afternoon," Mr. Warden told him. "We'll have to leave it to the doctor to decide when he sees Dusty tomorrow." Then he added, "Five extra points for Cabin 13 because you've carried on so well without your counselor." His departing footsteps crunched away down the path.

"Do you think we might get Top Cabin?" asked Kippy, in the darkness.

"No such luck," Boris predicted, "unless we can win a lot of races tomorrow. And Spider can't run, so . . ." He left his thought unfinished out of

116

politeness to the others, but everyone knew what he meant.

"We've still got you," Spider said. "You can win as many races as I can any day. And Kippy's fast." One by one they dropped off to sleep. Josh bore no resentment that no one considered him the possible winner of a race. His last thoughts were about Dusty's advice: "Run every race to win."

For that reason he went early the next day to the big field and practiced some starts before the track meet began. He also checked his shoelaces and tied double knots. Gradually the field filled with boys and counselors, all wearing badges, gray for Pioneers, green for Indians.

The first race was to be a hundred-yard dash for the seniors. Now, while everyone was fresh and rested, so many of the seniors wanted to enter that the race would have to be run off in heats. Everyone else sat or sprawled at the edge of the field, while counselors acting as judges and linesmen checked their stop watches and marked the start and finish lines with their tapes. The line marker from the tennis courts was being used today so that starts and finishes would be clear, definite, and official. There was no sign of Dusty. Josh would have liked to have Dusty see him win a race.

"What races are you going to enter?" Spider

asked, sitting down in the shade of a tree to protect his bald head.

"All of them," Josh said. It seemed to him that the seniors were taking a long time to run off all the heats of their hundred-yard dash.

"Golly!" said Spider. "Can you last?"

"Sure," Josh told him. "As well as anybody else."

Mr. Warden was speaking through a megaphone. "Juniors get your numbers for the fifty-yard dash." Josh stood up. "See you," he said. His heart was thumping as he trotted over to a table where one of the counselors was writing down names and handing out numbers. Cheers were coming from the sidelines as the senior hundred-yard dash ended. Mr. Warden announced the first-, second-, and third-place winners. More cheers. Someone was pinning a number on the back of Josh's T-shirt. "Cobb—number 23." A lot of juniors were entering the fifty-yard dash. As in the senior race, there would be several heats.

"Juniors at the mark!" Josh found his place and toed the mark. None of his special friends was in this heat. What had Dusty told him to do? He could not remember a word of it—except "Run every race to win." That he would do!

"Get set, go!" He heard shouting and felt his muscles straining, his lungs aching. The field heaved and flashed past under his feet. And suddenly there

was the finish line. He flung himself at the tape and kept running a good five yards past it.

He heard Mr. Warden's voice, "First place—Cobb!" He had done it. He had won a race. Of course, it was only the first heat, but he would win the finals too. He felt good and loose. His heart was still thumping, but not so hard now. Boris and Chatty were slapping his shoulder, punching his chest. He grinned vaguely and trotted off to the sidelines to rest.

"Good work," Spider said. "Now all you have to do is win the finals."

"I know," said Josh. He worked his arms and legs so that they would not get stiff. Then he stretched out on the grass.

While the next heat was being run off, someone sat down beside them. Josh turned and saw Dusty—Dusty looking pale and with dark circles under his eyes. He pulled up a long grass stem and began to chew it, squinting into the sun.

"How are you doing?" he asked.

"Josh won the first heat," Spider told him. "Didn't you see it?"

"I guess I just missed it," Dusty said. "I had to wait for the doctor. But I'll be here for the rest of the meet."

They were calling juniors for the potato race. Josh got to his feet.

119

"Let this one go," Dusty advised him. "Save your-self for the finals of the fifty-yard dash. They put in the potato race to give a breather to the finalists. Take advantage of it."

So Josh let the potato race go. He entered the sack race. Nobody took these two races very seriously and Josh did not feel really downcast when Boris won, crossing the finish line far in the lead, leaping like a kangaroo and never losing momentum. It was the kind of thing where good coordination counted, and Boris had that. Everyone was hooting and laughing as the other racers still humped and bumped and shuffled along the short course. Josh, having tried to overtake Boris with one mighty leap, had fallen flat once and sprawled headlong again as he crossed the finish line, barely nosing out the third racer. "First place—Morris! Second place—Cobb!"

Cabin 13 was living up to its reputation for speed. Josh and Boris helped each other out of their sacks and returned to the sidelines. Dusty nodded, looking pleased. "Good work," he said. They settled down to watch the broad jump and the high jump, which were senior events.

The high jump was still going on when Mr. Warden called, "Finalists for the junior fifty-yard dash!" Josh felt his nerves tingle. His stomach tightened. His mouth went dry.

"That's you," Dusty said. "Go on and win it."

120

Josh got to his feet. Stiff-legged, he walked to the starting line, eyeing the other five contestants. Mr. Warden's voice boomed through the megaphone, "First- and second-place winners of the three heats, Cobb, Foster, Thomas . . . Ferber, Goodman, and Woodruff." Josh had only time to see that Foster and Thomas were both bigger than he was and that both looked determined. His stomach tied itself into a knot.

"On your mark—" All six runners crouched. "Get set—" They raised themselves to the "ready" position.

"Go!" Josh launched himself out onto the course. It was a good start. He was running well, better than in the first heat. But the competition was better, too. He was running his best, arms at his sides, eyes on the finish line, giving the race everything he had, more than everything he had, and still, someone was pulling ahead of him. Was it Foster or Thomas? He did not know which was which. All he could do was to run his best up to and past the finish line, through a jumping, yelling crowd of boys. The tape was already broken. Someone had passed it before him.

"First place—Foster! Second place—Cobb! Third place—Thomas!"

Second place—Cobb. Josh went through the motions of shaking Foster's hand. (No question about which one was Foster now!) He shook Thomas' hand

121

too. Then he went off and was sick in the bushes.

Suddenly Dusty was there. "Don't worry about being sick. That often happens after a race. There's nothing wrong. Your stomach just tied up, that's all. You ran a nice race, Josh. Good boy!"

Josh did not answer. His stomach felt perfectly all right now and he was grateful for Dusty's help and reassurance. But he had lost the race. He had run that race to win and he had lost it anyway. That was all he knew.

On the field the hop, step, and jump was going on. "Don't enter this," Dusty said. "But try the three-legged race. Chatty wants to be your partner."

Josh nodded. His disappointment began to fade a little as Kippy thumped his back and Chatty stood up to help decide which of them should run on the left and which on the right in the three-legged race.

"Do you care whether we win?" asked Chatty.

"No, I don't care," Josh lied.

"That's good," Chatty said, "because I've never run much."

At those words Josh abandoned all hope of the three-legged race, but to his surprise he and Chatty almost won it. With his right leg tied to Chatty's left and with their arms across each other's shoulders, they were well matched in size. They managed to maintain a good rhythm along the whole length of the course, while most of the other pairs broke step,

pulled against each other, and seemed to take a step back for every two they took forward. The winners were Kippy and his small partner, whose speed and energy matched his own.

The Indians won the junior relay race without any trouble. The mere presence of Boris, Kippy, and Josh in the Indian lineup seemed to shake the confidence of the Pioneers. Speedy Spider was a Pioneer, but he was grounded, with his broken arm, under the tree on the sidelines. There was no question about it. Cabin 13, by pure luck, had more good runners than any other cabin in camp. Even Chatty, who was no runner and who did not care to win, had managed to get a second place in the three-legged race with the help of Josh. Cabin 13 was riding high.

The senior obstacle race, with its improvised hurdles and water trough, caused great joy among the spectators, and most of the campers left the field after that event. Only the die-hards stayed on to see the junior hundred-yard race, the last event of the track meet, and only a dozen junior campers stepped up to toe the mark. The others were all too tired. Chatty went to sit with Spider and Dusty under their tree. The three-legged race had been enough for him.

Josh, crouching at the starting line, could not see Boris or Kippy, but he knew that they were among the starters. He could hear Dusty's voice calling,

"Come on, Cabin 13!" This was his last chance to have Dusty see him win a race. He would run it to win. That was all he could do.

"On your mark! Get set! Go!" It was a good start. He was running well, not too tense. To left and right he could feel other runners on a level with him, but he did not turn to look. The finish line was at the end of the big field and he kept his eyes on it. It looked terribly far away. A few boys were gathered there with two counselors who must, he knew, be holding the tape. Off to the right someone was pulling ahead. Boris, or Kippy? No time to look now. His arms and legs felt like lead. He had a lump of lead in his chest. He thought of stopping, dropping out of the race. But even as he thought of this, he kept on running. Suddenly the boy on his left was no longer there. Without looking, Josh knew why. He was not the only one who was tired. That runner on his left had dropped out. Maybe someone else would drop out. Inside him, something said, "Keep going." His arms and legs got the message. The lump in his chest disappeared. The faces at the finish line were weaving and bobbing in front of him. He felt light and queer. He heard cheering and thought, "I've done it. I've won the race."

Then he heard Mr. Warden's voice echoing through the megaphone over the empty field, "First place—Thomas. Second place—Cobb."

124

THIRTEEN

Second Place—Cobb!

For the banquet after the track meet the dining hall was transformed into a place of splendor. Counselors had been working all afternoon, moving the tables to form something like a huge *B*. The head table was in its usual place, with the camp trophies standing on it, and the crossed paddles on the wall behind the table were decorated with balloons and horns. Other balloons and horns hung from paper streamers that crisscrossed in every di-

rection high above the tables. There would be a free-for-all to get them later on.

This was a night for ties and white shirts. From the kitchen came smells undreamed-of on ordinary nights, smells of roast beef and hot rolls and of chocolate pies. Those pies now stood in rows on the kitchen racks, ready to be topped with whipped cream at the last minute—regiments of pies, reserves enough to rush in second helpings or even third helpings for every boy in camp. Old Camp Buddy boys knew it and new boys guessed it.

Well before the dinner gong there was a crowd around the doors of the dining hall, and tonight no one was late. As the tables filled, all the festive touches were noted and duly appreciated. Quick-eyed Kippy pointed out the B-shaped table placement. Boris surveyed the trophies with hope. And Spider asked Josh to nab an extra balloon and horn for him. With his arm in the cast he did not think he could jump for them himself. Josh noticed again how much nicer Spider had been since his accident. Maybe a little trouble was good for some people! Chatty stood waiting for grace to be said. He knew that when everyone sat down they would find by each place a copy of the camp paper, *The Camp Buddy Breeze,* to which he had contributed a funny story, a poem, and a news report about the overnight hike. But no one would take time to read the *Breeze*

126

now. This was the time for eating. The special splendor of the occasion brought out traces of home table manners in a few campers, but no one was keeping track of table manners tonight.

When the chocolate pie had come and gone, melting away like snow in summer, Mr. Warden stood up. Counselors tapped on glasses with their forks and everyone quieted down.

"Fellow campers," Mr. Warden said, "we are celebrating tonight the end of a very good two weeks at Camp Buddy. For some of you it is the last night at camp. We will miss you." Groans and a few cheers. "Some of you are staying on for another two weeks." Cheers. "New campers will be coming tomorrow. You will know how to help them off to a good start in the Camp Buddy spirit."

Everyone at the Cabin 13 table exchanged glances, and Dusty nodded. They were all thinking about a telephone call that had come from Jumbo just before dinner. Jumbo's father had talked to Mr. Warden. Then Jumbo had talked to Josh and to Boris and Spider, all of whom had been summoned at top speed to the Director's Lodge for the purpose. As soon as Jumbo had got Josh's letter about the departure of Bert Bullock, he had told his father he wanted to come back to camp. Cabin 13 would help him get off to a good start this time.

Mr. Warden was concluding his speech. "This is

the moment for which you have all been waiting, the giving of awards and trophies. Not everybody will win an award. We all know that. The main thing is that you have all shown good sportsmanship in competition and have improved as campers."

Josh settled down to watch the winners go up to the head table in turn to receive their awards, clapping and cheering for each one. He felt a slight ache of disappointment that he had won nothing—nothing at all. But it was true, as Mr. Warden said, that the main thing was sportsmanship and improvement. His tennis was as bad as ever, because he had stayed away from the tennis courts as much as possible. Baseball was about the same. But without Bert Bullock to scare them half out of their wits, the scrub teams were doing better. If only he could stay two more weeks, Josh thought! Maybe he would surprise himself and everybody else by catching or hitting a ball before camp was over.

Spider was saying, "I might have been on the All-Stars if I hadn't broken my arm." Josh nodded. He was not the only one with a disappointment.

As for swimming, he had got out of the Tank and become a Sailfish. Silently, he determined to try his first dive tomorrow. Sooner or later would come the day when his fingers would close around the handle of a paddle. He could see himself pushing off across the lake into the light of the setting sun, "swift as the wild goose flies."

Now Mr. Warden was giving out the track awards. Again Josh felt a pang. It would have been great to win a race. There went Boris to get a blue ribbon. Josh clapped and cheered. There went Kippy . . . Another blue ribbon!

Then Mr. Warden was saying, "Second place, junior fifty-yard dash, Josh Cobb." Dusty pushed him to his feet. Josh blinked. He had been thinking hard about the blue ribbon he had *not* won, and he had forgotten the red ribbon he *had* won. There it was, being pinned to his shirt while he shook hands with Mr. Warden. He returned to his seat in the midst of prolonged applause. Cabin 13 had organized a special cheering section.

"The junior sack race—first place, John Morris." There went Boris again to get another blue ribbon. And a moment later Josh was returning to the head table himself for another red ribbon, the award for second place in the sack race.

He had almost forgotten, too, about taking second place with Chatty in the three-legged race, but they were called up together to receive red ribbons for that event. Everyone laughed when he returned from the head table for the fourth time with his red ribbon for taking second place in the junior hundred-yard dash. His chest bloomed with red ribbons. Josh grinned and waved to the general cheer that went up for him. But, if just one of those ribbons could have been blue!

Now Mr. Warden was calling the winners of the silver cups, the campers whose names would be engraved on the trophies to stand on the shelf above the head table. Only senior campers were honored in this way. One by one they were going up to shake hands with Mr. Warden. To Josh these trophy winners seemed part of another world. The awards of Cabin 13 were small potatoes by comparison with the Seabury Cup for the Senior Camper Who Has Contributed the Most to Camp Buddy, the Atwood Trophy for the Best All-around Athlete, the Swimming Trophy, the Tennis Trophy, the Track Trophy, the Baseball Bat for the Best All-around Baseball Player.

When Josh thought they must have run through every possible ribbon and cup, Mr. Warden began on Special Awards. These were silver stars and caused the greatest excitement of all, because no one could know ahead of time who would win them. There were stars for the campers who had scored highest in several activities. One of these was for the camper with the highest score at the track meet. Josh looked around, wondering who it would be.

"Josh Cobb," called Mr. Warden.

Josh's jaw dropped.

Dusty nudged him. "Go on and get it," he said. "Good boy!"

131

"But it can't be me," Josh sputtered. "I didn't win a single race."

"Go and get your star," Dusty insisted.

Stumbling over feet, his own and others, breathless and dazed, Josh made his way to the head table under a storm of applause.

Mr. Warden pinned a silver star to the pocket of Josh's shirt, where it shone among his red ribbons. "Josh won second place four times," Mr. Warden announced. "Second place counts three points. This gives him a total of twelve points which he scored at the track meet, more points than any other camper, junior or senior, at the meet."

Cabin 13 rose as one man, palms sore with clapping and throats hoarse with shouting to welcome the returning hero. After that, everything was a blur of final awards, a tangle of balloons exploding and horns hooting, until Taps sounded and silence fell on the exhausted camp.

"I still don't see how I got it," Josh said from his upper bunk.

"Because you entered more races than anyone else," Dusty told him as he fell into his own sleeping bag. "You placed high in every race you entered. You're what they call a consistent performer."

Josh lay with his hands clasped behind his head, thinking it over.

"Dusty," Kippy's voice came sleepily, "are you

going to finish *The Hound of the Baskervilles* tonight?"

"I thought everyone was too tired," Dusty said. But a chorus of indignant denials convinced him that Cabin 13 was wide-awake. He turned on his flashlight and pulled the book from under his pillow. Josh could see Dusty's face in the circle of light as he began to read.

When the weird hound had barked his last and Sherlock Holmes and Dr. Watson had disappeared into their English fog, he closed his book. The air at Camp Buddy was full of cricket song and Cabin 13 was well content.

"Dusty," said Kippy, "there's one thing I don't understand. Was there a dog in the hound?"

For a moment there was silence. Then Dusty said, "A hound *is* a dog, Kip."

"Oh," said Kippy. "Well, it was a great story. I really liked it a lot. But I just wondered."

The next morning Jumbo came back. According to his own account, he had spent the last week in a resort hotel with his parents. There had been plenty to eat, but no fun. He had missed the lake and the cabin, "and all like such." He arrived in time for swimming, and it was while they were getting into their swimming suits and talking, sixteen to the dozen, that a shout went up and down the line of cabins, "Fire on the campus!" A female must be

approaching. Josh looked out along the path and saw his mother walking toward Cabin 13. He ran down the steps to meet her. Then he was being hugged and kissed, a process he could not enjoy with the knowledge that many pairs of eyes were watching through the screens of the surrounding cabins.

"Didn't you get my letter?" he asked. "I want to stay at camp. Is that O.K.?"

"It's all right," she said, looking at him appraisingly. "I did get your letter, but I came anyway to see how you are. What a sunburn! Does it hurt?"

"No," Josh said briefly. "How long are you going to stay? I mean, I hope you can stay awhile."

"I am going to stay for lunch," she told him. "Mr. Warden invited me. He says a Mr. and Mrs. Jones are here too, and there will be a few other parents bringing new boys."

Josh breathed more easily. "That's all right, then. We're going swimming now. Do you want to see me swim?"

"I'd love to," she said. "Where do you swim?"

"Off the dock. But you can't come there," he added in alarm as campers began to emerge from cabins, heading down to the lake. "I'll find a place for you."

He led her to a tree stump where she could sit and look down on the lake without being too conspicuous. Boris ran past, then Kippy and Chatty. A mo-

Second Place—Cobb!

ment later came Spider and Jumbo and two grown-ups whose plumpness made them easy to identify as Jumbo's father and mother.

While the parents introduced themselves, the boys went off down the path. But Josh lingered just long enough to ask his mother, "Is it all right about Dusty? Can he come to visit us?"

"Of course he can," she said. "He must be quite a boy."

"He's not a boy," said Josh. "He's a man."

Then he ran off, passing the others on the long steep path. The soles of his feet were tough now. The pebbles did not hurt any more. He ran fast because he wanted his mother to see him dive in.